THE BOY WITH VIDEO GAME POWERS

By

R.L. Ullman

But That's
Another Story...
Press

For Matthew

Cover design and character illustrations by Yusup Mediyan.

Published by But That's Another Story... Press
Ridgefield, CT.

Printed in the United States of America.
First Printing, 2024.
ISBN: 978-1-953713-75-9
Library of Congress Control Number: 2024902820

DON'T MISS THE ADVENTURE!

Join my mailing list at rlullman.com!

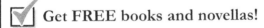 Get FREE books and novellas!

☑ Hear about new releases first!

☑ Join my Advance Reader Copy team!

☑ Save big on discounted book bundles!

☑ Check out fun book merchandise!

BOOKS BY R.L. ULLMAN

THE BOY WITH VIDEO GAME POWERS

The Boy with Video Game Powers
The Boy with Video Game Powers 2: Rescue Mode
The Boy with Video Game Powers 3: Tournament of Champions

EPIC ZERO

Epic Zero: Tales of a Not-So-Super 6th Grader
Epic Zero 2: Tales of a Pathetic Power Failure
Epic Zero 3: Tales of a Super Lame Last Hope
Epic Zero 4: Tales of a Total Waste of Time
Epic Zero 5: Tales of an Unlikely Kid Outlaw
Epic Zero 6: Tales of a Major Meta Disaster
Epic Zero 7: Tales of a Long Lost Leader
Epic Zero 8: Tales of a Colossal Boy Blunder
Epic Zero 9: Tales of a Souled-Out Superhero
Epic Zero 10: Tales of a Supremely Sore Loser
Epic Zero 11: Tales of a Mere Meta Mortal
Epic Zero 12: Tales of a Cosmic Catastrophe

MONSTER PROBLEMS

Monster Problems: Vampire Misfire
Monster Problems 2: Down for the Count
Monster Problems 3: Prince of Dorkness

UNLEGENDARY DRAGON

Unlegendary Dragon: The Magical Kids of Lore
Unlegendary Dragon 2: The Fall of Camelot
Unlegendary Dragon 3: The Battle for Avalon

TABLE OF CONTENTS

Chapter 1.	Game Over	1
Chapter 2.	Ring Me	14
Chapter 3.	Combat Mode	23
Chapter 4.	Power Boost	31
Chapter 5.	Public Enemy #1	40
Chapter 6.	Deathmatch	48
Chapter 7.	Call Me... Pixel Man?	55
Chapter 8.	Demon Spawn	65
Chapter 9.	House of Chaos	77
Chapter 10.	We Got Robbed	87
Chapter 11.	Reading Room Rumble	96
Chapter 12.	Disaster at the Dance	107
Chapter 13.	A Glitch in the System	115
Chapter 14.	Boss Battle	124
Epilogue	Press Start	137
Appendix	Milo's Level Up Chart	144

ONE

GAME OVER

I feel like I'm gonna be sick.

It's day one at my brand new school and I've finally reached the period I've been dreading the most.

Lunch.

The funny thing is, I told myself I wouldn't be "that kid." You know, the one who didn't make any new friends all morning and finds himself panicking over where he's going to sit at lunch. Yet, despite telling myself this, here I am, completely friendless and very much panicking over where I'm going to sit at lunch.

Universe, why art thou so cruel?

Okay, Milo, pull yourself together. After all, it's just lunch. It's not like you're moving in with these people. Besides, I probably look like a total dweeb just standing here with my lunch tray. So, I take a deep breath and survey my options.

To my left, a table of rowdy boys are engaged in an epic arm wrestling showdown. The grand prize of this senseless contest of strength is an impressively stacked mountain of brownies and a carton of hopefully still-in-date strawberry milk. I don't need to look at my scrawny arms to know that's not my table. Besides, I'm not giving up my brownie.

Next to them is a group of fashionably dressed kids who are texting so fast I think I see hashtags floating over the table. Sadly, despite how cool *I* think I am, I've never been mistaken for popular. My mom can't afford the latest clothes and I'm not allowed on social media. My one claim to fame was when I got pantsed in the middle of a school choir performance, but I'd rather not talk about that. Anyhoo, not my lunch spot.

To their right are a bunch of kids who look like they'd rather be studying in the library than hanging in the cafeteria. They're eating in complete silence as they flip through textbooks and mash buttons on calculators. For me, lunch is a break from school, not a chance to do more work. So, that's not my tribe either.

Gee, this is going well. Not.

Then, I spot a skinny kid sitting all alone at a table in the back. He's wearing a bright, red shirt and eating from a bagged lunch. His braces gleam as he smiles at me.

Well, that's the friendliest face I've seen all day, so here goes nothing. I smile back and navigate my way over, narrowly avoiding being conked in the head by a flying energy drink. But when I arrive, I notice a sign at the end of the table with big, bold letters that reads: ALLERGY TABLE.

"Oh," I say, stepping back. "Sorry, I didn't—"

"Don't go!" the boy exclaims, reaching out to me like he's been marooned on a deserted island. "I mean, please don't go," he says more calmly. "You're fine as long as you don't have peanuts. I'm allergic which is why I have to sit back here. I'm also allergic to lots of other stuff like dust, chihuahuas, and Christmas trees, but we can cover that later. Please, sit down. I'm Leon. Leon Williams. You don't have peanuts, do you?"

"Um, no," I say as I sit across from him. "I'm Milo. Milo Garret. I'm new here."

"Yeah, that's obvious," Leon says with a grin as he pulls a sandwich from his bag. "But don't worry about it, our whole grade is new here. School just started a few months ago."

Well, he's right about that. Truthfully, I never expected to be rocking my sixth grade year here at the prestigious Empire City Magnet School. All the best and brightest students from across Empire City go here from sixth grade through high school. I just never thought I'd be one of them.

I take a bite of my pizza which is uncomfortably chewy. Honestly, I never paid much attention to those state-level standardized tests we took at my old school. But to my surprise, I filled in enough bubbles correctly that they offered me a spot here even though the school year had already started. I didn't want to switch schools but Mom said it was an opportunity we couldn't pass up.

So, like it or not, here I am.

Of course, she's not concerned that it takes me three subways and over an hour to get here. Unfortunately, we live on the outskirts of the city in a neighborhood that's a little—okay, a LOT grittier than the posh neighborhood this school is located in. Just walking here from the subway station was like being in another world.

I'm used to cracked concrete, crumbling buildings, and 24/7 police sirens. But this area is the complete opposite, with beautiful brownstones, pristine streets, and green bushes. But that's not all that's different.

According to Mom, this school has a heavy STEM curriculum, which means I'll be learning more advanced stuff in science, tech, engineering, and math. I guess that's cool if you dream in code or have posters of periodic tables on your walls, but that's not my true passion. Nah, my true passion lies somewhere else.

"So, do you game?" Leon asks as he bites into his sandwich that's literally just two pieces of bread with nothing in the middle. Wow, I wonder what else this kid is allergic to.

"Yeah, you could say that," I answer casually.

Not to brag, but I'm kind of a big deal in the gaming world. In fact, I'm currently topping the leaderboards of several games, but my favorite is called—

"Ever play Ranger Quest?" Leon asks.

That's the one!

"All the time," I say with a big smile.

Ranger Quest is a massively multiplayer online game—also called an MMO—set in a sword and sorcery fantasy world where players create avatars to defend the land from evil. It has millions of players who are all trying to reach the highest level possible to gain new skills and earn awesome weapons and magical items.

"Same!" Leon says, perking up as he picks at a chunk of bread caught in his braces. "What level are you?"

"1,499," I say as I unwrap my brownie.

"What?!" Leon exclaims as the bread flies out of his mouth and lands on the table between us. "Yeah, right! There are only three players at that level and they're absolute legends. You've got ElfieMcElfFace221, BlueFuzzyFungusFoot99, and TheMighty…"

Suddenly, his voice trails off as he stares at me with his mouth hanging open.

"… Milo#1," I say, finishing his sentence. "Yep, that's me."

"No. Way," Leon says, sitting back in his chair. "You're TheMightyMilo#1? I can't believe it! I'm sitting with royalty! I'm only at level 233 which is nothing compared to you but… how'd you get so high anyway?"

"My mom is a police officer," I say. "So let's just say I've got plenty of time on my hands."

"That's incredible," Leon says. Then, he slaps the table and says, "Hey, isn't Ranger Quest releasing an ultra-rare mystery item this afternoon? Only the top players can play for it, and one of those players is you!"

"I know," I say. "And I've got a plan to get it first."

"Really?" Leon says, slurping his juice box. "Do tell."

"Sure," I say. "You see, I've got this special—"

"Well, well. What do we have here?" comes a deep voice from behind me. "A new loser at the loser's table?"

"T-Tank!" Leon squeals as his eyes go wide.

Tank? I look over my shoulder and see a gigantic kid with a crewcut, no neck, and enormous arms. Well, I can certainly see how Tank got his name. And he's not alone, because two equally large kids are snickering behind him.

"I want a soda, Williams," Tank grunts, taking the last bite of his banana. "Give me your debit card or else."

Well, will you look at that? I didn't realize that magnet schools also attracted bullies. Since I'm not big, strong, or particularly brave, I've had my share of problems with bullies in the past. But I'm not starting my new school going through that again. They say you've got to stand up for yourself, so I take a deep breath and...

"How interesting," I say, rising from my chair and turning toward Tank. "I didn't know they let kids go here who can't read."

"What are you blabbering about?" Tank asks as he throws his banana peel on the ground. "I can read."

"Really?" I say, picking up the sign from the table. "Well, if that was true then you'd know this doesn't say 'Loser's Table' but 'Allergy Table.' So, we'd appreciate it if you'd make like a tree and leave because my friend here and I both happen to be allergic to meatheads."

"M-Milo?!" Leon exclaims, his voice cracking.

Suddenly, I realize we've drawn a crowd! And more importantly, Tank isn't going away!

"Har dee har har!" Tank says as he leans into me, his foul-smelling banana breath going right up my nose. "Wanna know what I'm allergic to?"

"Um, toothpaste?" I say, swallowing hard.

"No," Tank says. "Wise guys."

Uh oh. I step back as he raises his giant fist, but my foot lands on something slippery and I'm suddenly falling backward—SMACK! Pain radiates through the base of my head and then everything... goes... black...

***

"Ow!" I exclaim as Ms. Rosario puts an ice pack behind my head.

"Mi pequeño Milo," she says with a sympathetic face as she adjusts her white ponytail. "Be glad it's not worse."

Well, that's true. Apparently, before Tank could clobber me, I slipped on his banana peel and hit my head on the table. The next thing I knew, I was in a police car heading to the hospital to see if I had a concussion.

Of course, the police car belonged to Mom and she was none too pleased that she had to leave her shift to get me. That was bad, but it's nothing compared to the lousy impression I made on my classmates. I'm probably the first kid in history to be knocked out by a banana.

At least Mom waited until I got a clean bill of health before she read me the riot act. On the ride home, I stared out the window while she fired rhetorical questions at me. Like: "Are you trying to waste this opportunity?" And: "Don't you see what you can become?" Then, she added one zinger that really got my goat: "Do you want to be like your father?"

I never knew my father. He abandoned us when I was a baby, so he's the last person I want to be like.

Since I didn't have a concussion, Mom dropped me off at Ms. Rosario's apartment and went back to work. Ms. Rosario lives next door and has watched me for as long as I can remember. She's a retired math teacher who makes some of the best food around. Sometimes when she's frustrated she'll mutter things she thinks I don't understand in Spanish. But I've translated a few of them on my phone and boy were they spicy!

I love Ms. Rosario. She's like the grandma I never had. Her cat, on the other hand, is like the pet I never wanted. He's a black cat who crossed our paths when Ms. Rosario found him on her fire escape. She took him in, named him Precious—or 'Precioso' in Spanish—and he's been trying to kill me ever since.

Don't get me wrong, I like animals but this cat clearly wants me out of the picture. He stalks me all over her apartment and attacks when I least expect it! Of course, Ms. Rosario is never around when he strikes, which I'm sure is all part of his nefarious plan.

Precious narrows his yellow eyes and glares at me as Ms. Rosario adjusts my pillow. I glare back when I notice the clock behind him. It's almost four o'clock!

Oh no! I've got an appointment I can't miss!

"Ms. Rosario, isn't Susurros del Pasado about to begin?" I ask. That's her favorite telenovela which means "Whispers From the Past" in English. From what I've seen, it should be called "Overly Dramatic Slop With Really Bad Actors."

"Yes, it is!" she says, looking at the time.

"Go ahead. I'll be fine," I say. "I'll game in here so you can watch TV in the living room."

Ms. Rosario's apartment is small, just like ours. It has a living room, a kitchenette, a bathroom, and two small bedrooms. I sleep in her spare bedroom whenever Mom has an overnight shift.

"Perfect, Milo," she says, brushing my cheek. "Precioso will keep you company."

Gee, isn't that wonderful news? As she exits, I notice him staring at me like I'm a fish dinner.

"Shoo," I say, waving him away. "I don't need your kind of company."

He hisses and slinks out of the room.

Great. Now I can game in peace.

I move to the desk and boot up my gaming laptop. I drop it off here every morning so I can play after school. Of course, Ms. Rosario makes sure I've finished all of my homework first, but today that's not an issue.

As the computer boots up, I look at myself in the mirror and shudder. There are circles under my brown eyes and my dark hair is plastered down in a tragic case of hospital bedhead. Just then, the screen flickers on and I click the 2D sword icon. Then, I see the following:

RANGER QUEST®
CREATED BY LORD CHAOS.
A CHAOS GAMES PRODUCTION.

Lord Chaos is my idol. No one knows much about him, including his real name, and he likes it that way. He's won tons of gaming awards but he never shows up to accept them. What I do know is that he's been around a long time. He started his career designing those old, stand-up arcade games my mom played as a kid. Then he developed some of the first console games before focusing entirely on online gaming. Ranger Quest is his biggest hit and it's probably made him a gazillionaire.

As the game opens, I focus on the task at hand. There's no way I'm letting someone else get this ultra-rare item. Of course, as a top player, I don't really need more things to dominate. But it's not about that.

In my daily life, I'm nothing special. I've never excelled in anything but school, and now I'm with tons of smart kids. But in Ranger Quest it's different. Here, I'm someone important, someone that people like Leon look up to. So, getting these items helps me stay on top.

Just then, my avatar appears on the screen. He's a knight decked out in a suit of enchanted armor and armed to the teeth with the best ranged and melee weapons in the game. In addition, at Level 1,499 I've nearly maxed out every single attribute available.

Strength: 100. Agility: 100. Stamina: 100. Intelligence: 100. Luck: 99. I also have crazy high Mana, and when I get this ultra-rare item, I'll be the first player to reach Level 1,500. Suddenly, a message pops up:

WELCOME ADVENTURERS!
THE ULTRA-RARE ITEM HAS BEEN RELEASED.
ONLY PLAYERS AT LEVEL 1,499 ARE ELIGIBLE
FOR THIS QUEST. THE FIRST TO GET THE ITEM
WILL BE THE ONLY ONE TO HAVE IT.
GOOD LUCK!

Here we go! Suddenly, a map of a maze-like dungeon appears and my avatar is sandwiched between a green elf and a blue, bearded sorcerer. Well, that must be ElfieMcElfFace221 and BlueFuzzyFungusFoot99. But as they take off in opposite directions, I hold my ground.

There's no need to scramble. I've got a plan.

I call up my Inventory Window and rifle through my items for the special artifact I've been saving for just such an occasion. The question is, where did I put it?

The Cloak of the Celestial Moon? No. The Gloves of Amarand? Nope. The Mystic Mirror Shield? Not it.

Aha! There it is! The Seeking Staff of Balidor.

I picked up this little beauty when I was the first to reach Level 1,000. This staff can detect the aura of any new magical item on the map. It's also a one-use item, so now is the perfect time to take it for a spin.

I equip it and go back to the map to find a directional arrow over my avatar's head. Awesome! If I just follow the arrows, they'll lead me straight to the ultra-rare item. I go flying by the elf. See ya, leotard legs!

As the arrows guide me through the dungeon's twists and turns, I plow through any creature who dares to spawn in my path. I debone skeletons, turn goblins into goop, and dice a legendary dragon into dragon McNuggets. Ah, it's good to be the king. Or at least, the king of Ranger Quest.

The arrows lead me through a hidden wall into a pitch-black room. Wow, it would have taken me forever to find it on my own. I equip my torch and prepare to battle a giant spider or vampire, but there's no one around. Instead, I see a golden altar with a chest on top.

That's got to be it! I pick the lock and open the chest to find a green, gleaming 2D ring! Hmm, for Level 1,500 I was expecting something way better than this. But when I pick it up, this message pops up:

Item:	Class: Ultra-Rare
Glitch Ring	Traits: To be determined

Huh? What does 'to be determined' mean? I've never seen that before. Then, another message flashes:

CONGRATULATIONS, CHAMPION!
YOU HAVE ACQUIRED THE ULTRA-RARE
GLITCH RING. USE IT WELL, FOR THE FATE OF
YOUR WORLD NOW DEPENDS ON YOU!

Cool, although the message is kind of confusing. Anyway, I look at my level, ready to do a happy dance as it jumps to Level 1,500. But instead, it resets to… Level 1!

Huh? What happened?!

Then, the screen flickers and shuts off!

"Milo!" Ms. Rosario calls out from the other room. "Your mother is here!"

"Milo?" Mom calls out. "Let's go. I've got dinner."

But I can't speak. Instead, I'm staring at the blank screen in disbelief. I mean, I've practically spent my entire life playing this game. If I just lost everything, I'm gonna rip my hair out!

"Milo?" Mom calls again. "Now please."

"Um, coming!" I call back.

I want to reboot but I can't right now. So, I grab my laptop, leap over a prowling Precious, and exit the room in a state of shock.

TWO

RING ME

My alarm BLARES, and when I open my eyes the sun is shining through my window blinds.

It was a long night, but somehow I managed to get some sleep. I rub my eyes. I still can't believe it's gone.

The game. My avatar. My life.

And it didn't just happen to me. Last night, the message boards were filled with people complaining about the same thing. It's like Ranger Quest completely disappeared from the face of the Earth!

I thought it would come back online eventually, but every time I clicked the sword icon nothing happened. I tried rebooting my computer, deleting and reinstalling the game, and even praying, but nothing worked.

I'm not gonna lie, I cried a little. Okay, I cried a lot. But I was beyond frustrated. I mean, I can't even tell you how many hours I've spent playing that game.

Mom hugged me and tried to tell me it was just a video game, but she's wrong. It was so much more than that. It was the best part of my life.

The alarm is still going which means it's time to get ready for school. But when I reach out to shut it off, I notice something gleaming on the pointer finger of my right hand.

Huh? What's that? I look at my hand, totally confused. It's… a ring?

It's green, shiny, and has gold circles, squares, and triangles running around it. That's weird. I don't wear rings.

So, where did this one come…

Suddenly, a chill runs down my spine.

No. It can't be. That's impossible.

Am I still sleeping? Is this a dream? I close my eyes and open them again, but the ring is still there! Maybe I hit my head harder than I thought yesterday. But as I run my fingers over the ring's embossed surface, it feels real, too real to be a figment of my imagination.

So, unless I've gone insane, which is entirely possible, that means that somehow, I'm wearing the Glitch Ring from the game—but in real life!

I try taking it off my finger, but I can't! No matter how hard I pull, it won't come off. It's stuck!

KNOCK! KNOCK!

"Milo?" comes Mom's voice. "Are you up, honey?"

"Um, yeah!" I call out quickly. "Wide awake!" The last thing I need is for her to come barging in right now.

"You need to get moving for school," Mom says. "Hit the shower and get dressed. I'll get breakfast ready."

"O-Okay!" I say, hearing my voice crack.

I wait for her footsteps to fade away and then rush into the bathroom. In the shower, I try loosening the ring with soap but it still won't come off! I don't know what to do about this ring but I do know one thing, I can't be late for school. I get dressed and meet Mom in the kitchen. As I enter, I cover my right hand with my left.

"About time," she says. She's dressed in her police uniform and sipping coffee from a big mug.

But when I look up, I stop dead in my tracks.

"Milo, what's wrong?" she asks, her brown eyes narrowing. "You look like you've seen a ghost."

I want to answer, but I can't because there's a transparent panel floating over her head with writing in bold, white letters. It says:

Hazel Garrett		Level: 1	
Strength: 9	Agility: 11		Stamina: 12
Intelligence: 12	Mana: 0		Luck: 0
Magic: None		Items: None	

That panel has the same attributes as the characters in Ranger Quest! But why is it floating over Mom's head?

"Earth to Milo," Mom says. "Come in, Milo."

"Um, what?" I say, looking into her eyes.

"Does your head still hurt?" Mom asks. "Should we go back to the hospital?"

"No, I'm okay," I say as I sit down at the table and take a spoonful of cereal. I'm about to eat it when—

"Where did you get that fancy ring?" Mom asks.

Ring? I look down and realize I'm holding my spoon with my right hand! Drat! Her stats panel distracted me and I forgot all about it! I've got to come up with something fast. Then, I see the cereal box.

"This cheap thing?" I say as I switch my spoon to my left hand and drop my right hand under the table. "It's from the back of a cereal box. I sent in three box tops as proof of purchase and they mailed it to me."

"Cool," Mom says, studying the back of the cereal box. "When I was a kid we could only get lame things like mini magnifying glasses and plastic watches."

"Speaking of watches, look at the time," I say, standing up. "I don't want to be late for school. Hopefully, my three subways are running on schedule."

"Look, Milo, I'm sorry it's so far away," Mom says as I grab my backpack. "You know I just want the best for you. Don't get me wrong, I enjoy being a cop, but sometimes I wonder what my life would have been like if I had gotten an opportunity like you have now." Then, she stands up and hugs me. "I love you, honey."

"I love you too," I say.

"Hey," she says, looking into my eyes. "Remember, life is a lot like those video games you play. The more challenges you face, the more chances you have to level up. You wouldn't hold yourself back from leveling up in a video game, would you?"

"No," I say.

"Well, this new school is an opportunity to level up in real life, so take advantage of it," she says with a gentle smile. "Now have a great day and this time let's try not to end up unconscious."

"I'll do my best," I say with a smile. I try to keep my cool but her stats panel is still hanging over her head.

"Oh," she says. "Don't forget to drop your gaming laptop at Ms. Rosario's so you'll have it after school."

"Will do," I say as I pick it up and head into the hall.

I knock on Ms. Rosario's door and wait for her to unlatch her ten bolt locks. When she finally opens the door, I see her smiling face and a transparent panel floating over her head!

Maria Rosario		Level: 1	
Strength: 4	Agility: 3		Stamina: 8
Intelligence: 10	Mana: 0		Luck: 0
Magic: None		Items: None	

"Buenos dias, Milo," she says. "I'll take your laptop."

"Um, th-thanks," I stammer.

As I hand it to her, I hear a MEOW from inside. I look over and see Precious perched on the back of the couch with a panel hanging over his head!

Precious		Level: 1	
Strength: 1	Agility: 20		Stamina: 5
Intelligence: 7	Mana: 0		Luck: 0
Magic: None		Items: None	

What's going on? And doesn't his Intelligence seem really high for a cat?

"Milo, is everything okay?" Ms. Rosario asks.

"What? Oh, yeah, everything is fine," I say. "I-I'll see you later." I fake a smile and head down the stairs since the elevator in our building has been busted for years.

Maybe I just need some fresh air. But as I exit onto the street, I see transparent panels floating over everyone's head! And when I mean everyone, I mean absolutely E-V-E-R-Y-O-N-E! Construction workers, cab drivers, store owners—even pigeons!

"Hey, Milo," Mrs. Maloney says as she hobbles past me on the street. Wow, her Stamina is surprisingly high for an old lady with a cane!

Then, a lightbulb goes off in my brain and I look down at the ring. What if I'm not going crazy? What if the Glitch Ring is making this happen? What if it's making the real world look like a video game?

The thought blows my mind, but if I don't get moving I'll miss my first subway and be late for school. I run to the Third Street Subway Station and race down the stairs. As usual, the platform is jam-packed with people. But now it seems even more crowded with all of the panels hovering over their heads.

Even though it feels like I'm invading their privacy, I can't stop looking at everyone's attributes. There's a young woman in a nice dress with a super high Strength rating, and a guy in a business suit who has incredibly low Intelligence. This is actually kind of fun!

Just then, a subway arrives but it's not mine. Ugh! I'm going to be late now. I wait on the platform as everyone loads into the cars and the subway takes off.

Suddenly, I'm alone.

"Welcome, Champion," comes a warm voice from behind that makes me jump.

I spin around to find an elderly man sitting on the floor next to a post. He's wearing a black, knit cap, a green jacket, and tattered jeans. His eyes are bright blue, and he has long white hair with a matching beard.

There were so many people in the station I didn't notice him before. And strangely, there's no panel floating over his head. Well, Mom taught me not to talk to strangers, especially in the subway station. But wait a second, did he just call me—

"Champion," the man says with a broad smile. "The fate of your world now depends on you."

He did call me Champion! And he just said the same thing the game said after I got the ring!

"Who-Who are you?" I ask, stepping back.

"I am Greylore," he says. "I am here to assist you with your quest."

"Quest?" I say confused. "What quest?"

"You are the Champion," Greylore says. "The only one worthy of wearing the Glitch Ring. And you must defend your world from the dangers of the Gameverse."

"The Gameverse?" I repeat. "What's that?"

"The Gameverse is a universe that exists in an alternate reality ruled by evil," he says. "For centuries, powerful forces have battled amongst themselves to expand their empires. But now they have discovered your reality—a reality filled with new lands to conquer and new subjects to enslave. And they will be arriving soon."

"Um, right," I say, pinching the Glitch Ring. "Look, I don't want this ring, so if you can take it off me and—"

"The ring belongs to you, Champion," Greylore says. "It grants you and you alone the power to stop the evil forces of the Gameverse before your world is destroyed."

Just then, my subway pulls into the station.

"Look," I say, backing up. "That's a great story and all but I'm late for school. So, I've really gotta—"

"You may run if you wish," he interjects, "but you cannot escape your fate."

The subway doors open and people get out.

"Ah," Greylore says, closing his eyes. "I sense your first challenge is upon us."

Huh? What's that supposed to—

Suddenly, a bright, blue light appears on the far end of the platform.

"Hey, what's that?" I hear someone say.

I have no idea. And why is it hovering in mid-air?

But before I can ask Greylore about it, the blue light starts swirling, churning faster and faster, expanding larger and larger, until it forms a big, blue circle.

Then, a skeleton leaps out!

"Aaahh!" a woman screams.

It takes a second for my eyes to register what I'm seeing because this is no ordinary skeleton. This one is very much alive, and it's carrying a sword and shield!

"GRAAARRR!" it bellows, its shrill voice echoing through the station as the blue portal behind it disappears into thin air.

"So, Champion, what will it be?" Greylore asks calmly. "Will you go to school, or will you fulfill your destiny?"

THREE

COMBAT MODE

I knew I should have stayed in bed.

First, I wake up with the Glitch Ring on my finger. Then, a homeless guy calls me "Champion" and tells me I'm the only one who can stop evil forces coming from an alternate reality called the Gameverse. The next thing I know, a skeleton with attitude problems is spawning right here in the subway! And to top it off, I'm late for school!

Yet as people flee for the exits, I feel a strange sense of calm. Although my head is telling me to run, something in my gut is making me stay. All the while, the skeleton is lumbering toward me, one step after another, like it's learning to walk all over again.

"Behold your first challenge, Champion," Greylore says. Despite the advancing skeleton, he doesn't look concerned at all. In fact, he's still sitting on the dirty floor. "Will you choose to run or fight?"

Fight? I can't fight that thing! Then, I realize the skeleton has a panel hanging over its head too, but this one has some different info than the ones I saw before.

UNDEAD SKELETON		
Challenge Level: Easy		XP: 25
Strength: 8	Agility: 5	Stamina: 6
Intelligence: 3	Mana: 0	Luck: 0
Magic: None	Weapons: Basic Long Sword; Basic Iron Shield	

According to this, it's rated "Easy" for Challenge Level, and destroying it is worth 25 XP, otherwise known as Experience Points. Suddenly, I realize I've seen these stats before. This skeleton is just like the ones in Ranger Quest! I've killed thousands of them in the game!

"What is your decision, Champion?" Greylore asks. "If you allow it to leave this station, it will attack the innocent citizens of Empire City."

Yikes! I guess I don't have a choice!

"How can I fight it when I don't have any weapons?" I ask. And now it's only twenty feet away!

"Ah, but you do," Greylore says with a smile. "Just open your Inventory."

"My… Inventory?" I say confused.

"Yes, simply focus your mind and call up your Inventory Window," he says. "That is where you will find all of the items currently in your possession. It is also where you can store any items you collect for future use. All you need to do is concentrate."

"I know what an Inventory Window is," I say, "I just didn't realize I had one." I close my eyes and focus on pulling it up. When I open my eyes again, I see a 2D grid floating in front of me! Whoa. That's cool.

The grid is empty except for two slots in the upper left. One has a 2D icon of a silver suit of body armor and the other has a 2D icon of a sword. There's also a grid in the lower right corner that says "Spells," but it's empty.

"Good," Greylore says. "Now select an item to read its description and then you can mentally equip it."

Um, okay. I select the armor and read the information that appears beside it:

Item:	Class: Common
Flexible Plate Armor Skin	Traits: +10 Defense

Flexible Plate Armor Skin? Ranger Quest had plate armor, but it wasn't flexible. I mentally equip it, and I'm suddenly encased in snug body armor from head to toe! I look at my armor-plated hands through the narrow eye slits of my helmet. The armor is covering the Glitch Ring, and my hands look strangely pixelated, just like in the game.

I run a hand across the tiny air holes around my mouth and nose. Good, I can breathe. Next, I bend my arms. Wow, this armor really is flexible. But now the skeleton is only five feet away!

"You will need your sword," Greylore suggests.

Right! I go back into my Inventory and select it.

Item:	Class: Common
Basic Long Sword	Traits: +10 Attack

Well, it's not exactly the Singing Blade of Blackraven but it'll have to do. I mentally equip it and I'm suddenly holding a sword in my right hand that's so heavy it throws me off balance!

"Good luck, Champion," Greylore says.

"Hey, aren't you going to help me?" I ask.

"I am afraid that is not my role," he says, folding his hands in his lap.

"AAARRRGGGHHH!"

Uh oh! I turn and the skeleton is right in front of me with its sword raised over its head! Before I can move, it slashes down at me, and—CLANG—the blade strikes me hard on my left shoulder, knocking me backward!

Ow, that hurt! Thank goodness I'm wearing armor because if I wasn't I'd be a goner! But then, a new transparent bar appears that says:

Health	90/100

"Um, what's that?" I ask.

"That is your Health Status Indicator," Greylore says. "You start with full health, but when you are hit by magical or non-magical attacks, your health will decline until it reaches 0. When that happens, you will die."

"Wait, what?!" I say.

"This is not a game where you have the luxury of multiple lives," Greylore says. "In your reality, you only have one life and you must protect it at all costs. But do not worry, with adequate rest your body will be restored to full health."

Rest sounds nice. But clearly, I'm not going to get it right now because the skeleton takes another swing at me!

This time I lift my sword and—CLANG—block it.

This is nuts! I'm not only sword-fighting a skeleton in the subway station, but now I can actually see when I'm about to die!

"GRRRAAARRR!" the skeleton roars.

Okay, I've had just about enough of this guy. Time to put my Ranger Quest skills to use. I raise my sword and slice down, but—CLONK—the skeleton blocks it with its shield! I spin around and thrust at its exposed ribcage but—KLONG—it blocks that too!

"This creature is one of the lower-level foes you will face," Greylore says rather unhelpfully.

What gives? I mean, these things are easy to kill in the game, so how come it's so hard now? Maybe it's because I've never been in a real swordfight before. I mean, it's not like they teach us this stuff in gym class.

The skeleton jabs at me and I barely avoid being shish kabobbed. That's it. It's time for some real strategy.

"Hold onto your ribs, bonehead," I say, "because your whole world is about to fall apart!"

I fake an overhead strike and the skeleton raises its shield to parry. Then, I spin around and—BONK—hit its cranium with the base of my hilt and—SWOOSH—slash straight through its midsection! The skeleton collapses into a pile of bones! Yes! I did it!

Just then, a message pops up:

```
Enemy Vanquished:
You have gained 25 XP!
```

"Is that for real?" I ask. "Did I really just gain 25 Experience Points in real life?"

"Indeed," Greylore says. "When you defeat enemies, you gain Experience Points. When you gain enough XP, you can level up and increase your attribute scores. But beware because as you increase in level, the strength of your enemies will increase as well."

Suddenly, there's a flash of white light and the skeleton is gone! But in its place are two small gems—a green one and a blue one.

"Are those what I think they are?" I ask.

"Yes," Greylore answers. "They are items your enemy has dropped. The more you increase your Luck attribute, the greater the chance you will find items that may be of use to you."

This is incredible. I pick up the gems and stare at them in my hand.

Then, a panel appears that says:

> You have found:
> 1 Green Gem of Healing (+10 Health);
> 1 Blue Gem of Temporary Strength (+40 Strength)!

"Awesome!" I say. "But how do I use them?"

"Just place them in your Inventory and equip the item of your choice," Greylore says.

I concentrate and drop them into my Inventory grid. Then, I equip the green gem. Suddenly, my Health Indicator pops up and shows me back at full health. I rotate my left arm and my shoulder feels great.

"That's amazing," I say. "It feels like nothing happened."

"Very good," Greylore says. "Now take a moment to familiarize yourself with your starting status."

My starting status? That's funny, I got so used to seeing everyone else's statuses that it never occurred to me that I'd have one of my own!

"Just concentrate and call it up," Greylore advises.

Right. I focus and call up my Status Window.

MILO GARRETT		
Level: 1	XP: 25	Next Level: 50 XP
Strength: 7	Agility: 10	Stamina: 7
Intelligence: 13	Mana: 0	Luck: 5
Magic: None		
Items: Flexible Plate Armor Skin; Basic Long Sword; Blue Gem of Temporary Strength		

I'm only at Level 1. I see the 25 XP which are my current Experience Points, so I need another 25 XP to reach Level 2 at 50 XP. I check out my other attributes which aren't all that impressive, but at least I'm smarter than Precious.

Then, I notice I have 0 Mana. Mana is the attribute that lets you use Magic in Ranger Quest. Every spell requires a certain number of Mana points to use it.

"Can I use Magic?" I ask.

"Not yet," Greylore says. "But as you level up, it will become possible for you to use spells."

"Whoa," I say. "So, I'll have to defeat more enemies to level up. Are more coming?"

"Not at the moment, but they will," Greylore says ominously. "And when they do, you now know how to use the power of the Glitch Ring to protect your world."

"I guess so," I say as I call up my Inventory Window and put away my sword and armor.

Then, I realize something.

"Hey, was this some sort of a training session?" I ask. "Did you bring that skeleton here just to teach me what to do?"

Just then, I hear RUMBLING.

I turn to see my subway leaving the station, and when I look back at Greylore for his answer, he's gone.

FOUR

POWER BOOST

Needless to say, I'm late for school.

In fact, I'm so late the security guard has to buzz me into the building. Then, I have to check in with the front office before I can even go to class! I nearly fall over when the lady behind the desk says she has to call Mom to tell her I'm tardy. I beg her not to, but she just shrugs her shoulders and says it's school policy.

Great. Mom is going to flip out! But it's not my fault. I mean, I didn't plan on fighting a skeleton on my way to school! Unfortunately, I can't tell her that.

I tug at the Glitch Ring but it still won't come off. I can't believe I'm stuck with this thing. According to Greylore, this ring gives me the power to protect the world from evil coming from a place called the Gameverse—or die trying!

I don't know who Greylore was, but he sure knew a lot about the Glitch Ring. Unfortunately, he disappeared before he could answer my questions. So, I've been pretty distracted all morning, including in gym class.

"Mr. Garrett, please go to your side!" comes a gruff voice that echoes through the gym.

Huh? I snap back to reality and realize I'm standing at halfcourt while all of the other kids are standing on opposite sides of the gym.

"It's time for dodgeball, Mr. Garrett, not daydreaming," Mr. Stanley, our gym teacher says.

Great. Dodgeball. A game of torture designed for the amusement of gym teachers nationwide.

"Milo, over here!" Leon calls out.

As I run over, I see his stats floating over his head.

Leon Williams	Level: 1	
Strength: 5	Agility: 8	Stamina: 7
Intelligence: 14	Mana: 0	Luck: 0
Magic: None	Items: None	

Wow, Leon is smarter than me. I join him as Mr. Stanley starts barking instructions.

"Can you believe what happened to Ranger Quest?" Leon whispers. "It's as dead as a doornail."

"I know," I whisper back.

"Did you ever get that mystery item?" he asks.

"Yeah, you could say that," I whisper back.

"Garrett! Williams! Quiet!" Mr. Stanley shouts.

"Yo, Garrett!" comes a familiar voice from across the gym. Then, I see Tank on the other team. He makes a slashing motion across his neck.

I swallow hard and look at his stats:

Timmy Tankowski		Level: 1	
Strength: 13	Agility: 11		Stamina: 13
Intelligence: 11	Mana: 0		Luck: 0
Magic: None	Items: None		

Oh my, isn't he a strong one?

"Okay, students," Mr. Stanley shouts, "let the carnage begin!" Then he raises his whistle to his mouth and—TWEEEET!

Leon and I stand there as the other kids scramble to pick up dodgeballs and chuck them at the other team.

"You any good at this?" I ask Leon.

"Do I look like I'm any good at this?" Leon replies, squeaking as a dodgeball WHIZZES by his head.

THUMP! THOOP! THUNK!

Suddenly, all the kids on our team are mowed down until Leon and I are the only ones left! And when I look at the other side, Tank and his minions are still standing.

"I got a week of detention because of you losers," Tank says with a mischievous grin. "It's payback time!"

Then, Tank and his friends let loose! Somehow, I avoid getting hit, but Tank's dodgeball is heading straight for—SMASH! I cringe as the ball strikes Leon square in the forehead and he falls straight back.

"Leon!" I call out, kneeling beside him. "You okay?"

"Oh, I'm just fine, Mother," Leon says with a smile, his eyes completely glazed over. "Now would you be a dear and help me organize my butterfly collection?"

"Har har!" Tank snorts. "You're next, Garrett!"

The kids start chanting, "Get him! Get him!"

Great. The gym just turned into a gladiator arena and I'm the lion's snack!

Then, I see a pretty girl with long, red hair who isn't chanting with the others. Her arms are crossed and she looks disgusted by the whole spectacle.

I stand up as Tank and his goons take aim. Then, they all throw at once!

WHIZZ! WHOOSH! WHOOM! I dive left and do a somersault. Miraculously, I don't get hit.

"Don't worry, Garrett," Tank says as he picks up another ball. "We'll get you. It's just a matter of time."

He's right about that because it's three against one. But then I remember that I can even the odds. I pick up a dodgeball, open my Inventory Window, and find the item I'm looking for.

Item:	Class: Uncommon
Blue Gem of Temporary Strength	Traits: +40 pts of Temporary Strength

That's just what the doctor ordered! I mentally equip the blue gem and feel a strange, tingly sensation run through my body. Did it work? I sure hope so because one of Tank's buddies is lining me up for the kill!

Well, here goes nothing.

Before he can fire, I rear back my arm and throw the dodgeball with everything I've got.

FWOOM!!!

The ball blazes out of my hand like it was shot from a cannon and—POW—nails the kid square in the gut! Everyone watches as his body flies twenty feet through the air and THUDS against the far wall. Then, he crumples to the floor and doesn't get back up.

The whole gym goes silent.

I look at my arm. Whoa.

Then, I hear footsteps and spot Tank's other buddy racing for the exit.

I grab another dodgeball, measure the distance, and let it fly. The ball rockets across the gym and—BOOM— pegs him in the back, knocking him face-first to the ground. The kids cheer!

I grab a third dodgeball. It's Tank time.

"Hey, take it easy, Garrett," Tank pleads as he drops his dodgeball. "Look, I'm not even playing anymore. Let's just call it a draw, okay?"

I look into Tank's scared eyes. As much as I want to pummel him, I can't. He's unarmed.

"Fine," I say, showing him my dodgeball. "But if you bug me or Leon again, you'll be sorry." Then, I drop the ball and turn to check on Leon.

"Look out!" the red-haired girl shouts.

Huh? I spin around and duck just as Tank's dodgeball WHIZZES over my head.

That creep! I should have known. I pick up my dodgeball and hear—

TWEEEEETTTTT!

"That's enough, Garrett," Mr. Stanley says as he races over and puts his arm around my shoulder. "You know, you have quite the arm there. Have you ever considered trying out for the baseball team? I'm the coach here and…"

But I'm not listening to him. Instead, I'm looking at Tank who's smirking at me.

***

After gym class, I helped Leon to the nurse's office. Luckily, aside from the dodgeball-sized mark on his forehead, he was okay. Tank kept his distance during lunch, but I noticed him staring at me from across the cafeteria. I have a sneaking suspicion this isn't over, and that has me very, very worried.

My afternoon classes were pretty routine, and when the final bell rang I was happy to be heading home. On the positive side, I made it through a full day. On the not-so-positive side, Mom texted me about being late this morning. The fact that it included an angry-faced emoji probably wasn't a good sign.

As I exit the school to begin my long trek home, I see that red-haired girl from gym class standing on the corner. I noticed that she's in my science class too.

Over her head is her stats panel:

Claire Donovan		Level: 1	
Strength: 6	Agility: 10		Stamina: 7
Intelligence: 15	Mana: 0		Luck: 0
Magic: None		Items: None	

Wow, she's super smart. She's on the way to my subway station, so there's no way to avoid her. As I get closer, she sees me and brushes a strand of hair away from her face.

Suddenly, I feel nervous. Should I say something? If she doesn't respond I'll look like a total goober. Besides, why would she want to talk to me?

So, I stare at the pavement and keep moving.

"Um, hey," she says suddenly.

I stop, my eyebrows arching. "Sorry, were… were you talking to me?" I ask.

"Yes, I'm talking to you," she says, looking at me like I have two heads. "I just wanted to tell you that what you did in gym class was amazing."

"Oh," I say, surprised. "Thanks."

"I didn't think you could throw like that," she says. "You know, because you're not big or athletic looking."

"Gee, thanks, I think," I say. I try to look casual but realize my arms are crossed so I drop them to my sides.

"Sorry, I didn't mean it like that," she says. "It's just that Tank is a bully and I've never seen anyone stand up to him like that."

"Well, I probably wouldn't even be standing at all if it wasn't for you," I say. "So, thanks for the warning."

"No problem," she says. Then, she smiles, extends her hand, and says, "I'm Claire."

"Milo," I say shaking her hand. It feels warm.

"Nice to meet you, Milo," she says with a smile. "Cool ring," she says, pointing to the Glitch Ring.

"Oh, um, thanks," I say, realizing I used my right hand. I quickly stuff it into my pocket.

Just then, a black, stretch limo pulls up to the curb.

"Well, here's my ride," she says.

"That's your ride?" I say amazed.

"Yeah," Claire says as she opens the back door. "It's kind of embarrassing actually. Well, it was nice to meet you, Milo. See you around."

"Yeah, see you around," I say.

She gets into the limo and waves as it pulls away.

"Dude," Leon says, appearing out of nowhere. "Do you know who that is?"

"Claire," I say.

"Not just Claire," Leon says, "Claire Donovan! Her family is loaded. A limo drops her off every day. And her notebooks smell like rose petals."

"Well, she seems nice," I say. "And why are you smelling her notebooks?"

"Um, no reason," Leon says quickly. "Anyway, do you want to grab some ice cream? Normally, I can't have it but I heard there's a place down the block that serves dairy-free chocolate that supposedly tastes like the real thing. Not that I've ever tasted the real thing because I'm allergic to chocolate."

"That sounds like fun but maybe another time," I say, squeezing my ring. "I've got to go. There's, um, someone I need to see."

FIVE

PUBLIC ENEMY #1

Greylore is nowhere to be found.

He wasn't in the subway station or anywhere else I searched either. It's like he vanished into thin air!

And that's bad news for me.

He's the only one who knows what's going on and I need answers. Like, for instance, how I can get rid of this Glitch Ring. If the world is counting on me to save it, then it has another thing coming. After all, I still sleep with a night light!

The sooner I find Greylore, the sooner I can get my life back to normal. But by the time I reach my apartment building, it's dark out. I consider doing one last lap to find him, but it's not safe to wander around my neighborhood after dark.

Besides, I texted Ms. Rosario that I was working on an after-school project and I'd be home before dinner. I feel bad about not telling her the truth, but technically I wasn't lying because finding Greylore *was* my after-school project. But I don't want her to worry so I head inside.

As I climb the six flights of stairs and knock on her door, I think about how much I'd love to play Ranger Quest right now. Sadly, that's no longer an option. I wait for Ms. Rosario to unlock her security bolts and—

"Hola, Milo," she says with a big smile as she opens the door. "How was your project?"

"Not great," I say as I enter. Just then, Precious leaps onto the back of the couch and fixes me with a menacing glare. "Precious," I say with a nod and a clear warning in my voice, but he just yawns and licks his paw.

"I'm sorry your project didn't go well," Ms. Rosario says. "Would you like something to eat?"

"Um, no thanks," I say. "I'm not hungry. I think I'll go to the bedroom and get some… rest?"

I freeze. On Ms. Rosario's television, a news anchor is speaking in Spanish in front of the Third Street Subway Station. Behind him, I see sirens, yellow caution tape, and lots of police officers milling about.

"Um, what's going on?" I ask Ms. Rosario.

"What?" she says, looking at the TV. "Oh, they just shut down the Third Street Station. Apparently, something strange happened this morning and they're investigating it now. It's been all over the news."

Something… strange?

"Move over, cat," I say, shooing Precious as I grab the remote and sit down on the sofa. I'm not fluent in Spanish, so I switch to an English-speaking news channel where a female anchor is reporting.

"—unusual series of events," the reporter says. "This footage was captured at the Third Street Subway Station by a woman on her cell phone during the morning commute. If you have not yet seen this video, be prepared to be astonished."

The image switches to inside the station and I'm watching that swirling blue light from this morning! The video quality is poor, but I'm transfixed as I watch the light form into a circle—and then a skeleton steps out!

"As you can see, as if by Hollywood magic, a skeleton appears out of nowhere," the reporter continues, "and it does not look friendly. But don't turn the channel just yet because there's more."

More? My stomach sinks. Did the woman catch me on camera too? If Mom sees me fighting the skeleton, she's gonna kill me!

Then, someone wearing silver, pixelated body armor and carrying a long, pixelated sword jumps into the scene!

Who's that? But then it dawns on me.

That's me!

"Suddenly," the reporter continues, "this oddly costumed, unidentified person intervenes to fight the skeleton. Police believe this individual is a real person who is using an advanced blocking signal to distort their appearance on camera. And while this battle may look real, police believe this is likely just a publicity stunt for a movie or a social media influencer."

What?

That's not true!

As the battle with the skeleton heats up, other bystanders force the woman taking the video to go upstairs for her safety, and the video ends abruptly.

"If you have any information about the actors in this video," the reporter says with a smile, "please contact the Empire City Police Department. As you can imagine, they are very interested in speaking with them."

I turn off the TV and sit back in shock.

***

I spent the rest of my time at Ms. Rosario's watching myself on every single channel. And when I say every single channel, I mean EVERY. SINGLE. CHANNEL. And that includes news channels, foreign language channels, sports broadcasts, and cartoon networks!

Suddenly, I'm a viral sensation! Luckily, no one knows it's me, including Mom, which is a huge relief considering what she has to say about it during dinner.

"Whoever he is," Mom says as she takes a bite of fried chicken, "he's a menace."

"A menace?" I say surprised, pausing before I eat my mashed potatoes. "Um, what do you mean?"

"You saw the video," she says. "Some whacko is running around the city with a sword. That's dangerous."

"I guess," I say, lowering my fork. "But you heard what they're saying. It's probably just a movie stunt."

"Uh uh," Mom says, shaking her head. "That's just what we're telling the media to say, but it's not the truth."

"It's not?" I ask.

"Nope, not by a long shot," Mom says. "Not according to the FBI."

"The… FBI?" I say, my voice rising.

"Yep," Mom says as she grabs another piece of chicken. "It took a while for their experts to analyze the footage and interview all of the witnesses, but they believe everything in that video is real."

"R-Real?" I stammer. "W-What do you mean?"

"I mean everything," she says, peeling off some chicken skin. "The blue portal, the skeleton creature, the guy with the sword. All real."

"Y-You're kidding?" I say, my voice cracking. "Do they, um, know who the guy with the sword is?"

"No," she says. "Unfortunately, the security cameras inside the station weren't working so they couldn't get a good look at him. All we have is that woman's video."

"Oh, that's too bad," I say relieved.

"Listen, Milo, I'm telling you this because I want you to be careful," Mom says. "If something like that can happen in the subway, then it can happen anywhere. Of course, everything I'm telling you is confidential. You can't say anything about this to anyone."

"Believe me, I won't tell a soul," I say. "But, um, where do they think the kid with the sword, I mean, the person with the sword, came from?"

"Well, that's the million dollar question, isn't it?" she says, picking a small bone out of her teeth. "There are plenty of theories. Holograms. Aliens. But there's one theory that just keeps coming up."

"Oh?" I say, trying to sound casual. Then, I realize I'm resting my chin on my ring hand so I quickly drop it under the table. "And, um, what's that?"

"An alternate universe," Mom says. "Now don't look at me like that. I'm just telling you what I heard."

"You're joking," I say with a nervous smile. "The FBI actually thinks they're from another dimension?"

"Something like that," Mom says. "I don't believe it myself but we'll know more once they finish scrubbing the area."

"Scrubbing the area?" I say. Suddenly, I feel a pit in my stomach. "You mean, like, for fingerprints?"

"Exactly," Mom says. "If there's evidence to be found, the FBI will find it."

"How wonderful," I say, swallowing hard.

"They'll help us catch those guys so we can put them behind bars for a long, long time," she says.

"Right," I say. "But what if the guy who fought the skeleton isn't bad? I mean, what if he's like a hero or something? What if he was just trying to save the city?"

"Then he's a vigilante," Mom says. "You can't take the law into your own hands, and you certainly can't walk around the city wielding a sword and putting people in harm's way. But trust me, he's no hero and we'll get him one way or another." Then, she picks up a bowl and says, "Want some coleslaw?"

"Um, no thanks," I say, pushing back from the table. "If it's okay, I think I'll just get ready for bed."

"Me too," she says. "Today was crazy. I've got the night off but I'm exhausted. Do me a favor and clear your plate. And remember, don't tell anyone about this."

I smile and bring my plate to the sink. Then, I hug Mom, head into my room, and close the door.

My head is spinning as I flop onto the bed. I can't believe the FBI is involved! I mean, I've seen the crime shows. What if I left behind a sneaker print, or worse, my fingerprints? It's only a matter of time before they discover it was me! Mom will be so upset when they knock on our door and haul me away.

Just then, I notice a green light flashing by my side, and when I raise my right arm, the Glitch Ring is blinking! Oh no. What now?

I open my Inventory and don't see anything unusual. But then I notice a new 2D icon in the lower right corner.

It's a globe, and it's blinking!

I mentally select it and a giant map opens in front of me. As I study it, I realize it's a map of Empire City! And it has two flashing dots!

The green dot is located over my building, so that must be me. But the red dot is blinking right in the middle of Central Square—the busiest tourist section in the city! I click on the red dot and get this message:

AN ENEMY HAS SPAWNED!

Um, what? An enemy has… spawned?

I click the message to get more information but there's nothing. Great. Maybe it's another skeleton. But then again, maybe it's much, much worse.

For a second, I consider ignoring it. After all, the last thing I want is for Mom to find out that I'm the vigilante with the sword. But then I remember what Greylore said.

According to him, I'm the Champion, which means that I'm the only one who can stop this thing—whatever it is. And if I don't, people will get hurt.

Of course, I could get hurt too—even killed! I check my Health Status Indicator which reads: 100/100.

That's good and before I know it, I'm standing up and opening my bedroom window. I hesitate for a moment and look back at my closed bedroom door.

I sure hope Mom is sleeping.

Then, I step through the window and climb down the fire escape.

SIX

DEATHMATCH

Central Square, my least favorite part of the city.

Sure, I get that it's the heart of Empire City and attracts millions of tourists every year. But to me, it's a sensory overload nightmare.

The place is always swarming with people, you're bombarded by flashing lights everywhere you look, and it's so loud you can't hear yourself think. My life would be perfectly fine if I never stepped foot in Central Square again. But tonight I don't have that choice.

Of course, getting here was an odyssey. To avoid the FBI, I had to skip the Third Street Station to catch a subway on Eighth Street. By the time I arrive, the normal chaos of Central Square is at a whole new level because thousands of people are running for their lives!

Whatever spawned here must be bad because I have to hug a lamppost to avoid being crushed by the oncoming crowd! I try to find the source of the commotion but I can't see over the throngs of people. It's times like these that I resent being short!

Then, I spot a taxi flying through the air.

Bingo! That came from over there! I steel myself and push through the sea of humanity. Along the way, I hear snippets of conversation like:

"Did you see that monster?"

"It came out of nowhere!"

"Hey, where's that dumb kid going?"

I ignore that last one and keep moving. When I finally break through the crowd, I'm all alone in the middle of Central Square which looks like a war zone. Everywhere I turn, I see bashed cars, busted billboards, and shattered windows. But there's no sign of any—

"GGGRRRAAAGGGHHH!"

I spin around and my knees go weak because there, standing right across the street, is a gigantic, horrific-looking creature. He must be ten feet tall, with beige, wart-covered skin, bulging muscles, and a broad, sloping face. As he stares me down with his red, beady eyes, he effortlessly hoists a massive, spike-studded club over his shoulder.

I swallow hard. Well, now I know why everyone was running. I quickly look at the transparent panel floating over his head, which reads:

OGRE		
Challenge Level: Moderate	XP: 50	
Strength: 25	Agility: 9	Stamina: 22
Intelligence: 4	Mana: 0	Luck: 0
Magic: None	Weapons: Great Club	

An ogre? These brutes were in Ranger Quest too, and they're not easy to beat! Just then, his nose starts twitching like crazy. Great, either he's enjoying the stench of Central Square or he just got a big whiff of the fear wafting from my body.

Something tells me it's the latter.

"KILL!" he grunts with a deep, rumbling voice that rattles my bones. "KILL FOR NIKADEMOS!"

Nikademos? Who's that?

But I don't have time for questions because the ogre is charging at me!

THOOM! THOOM! THOOM!

His footsteps shatter the pavement as he raises his giant club over his head! Time to armor up! I open my Inventory Window, equip my Flexible Plate Armor Skin, and barely dive out of the way before—SMASH!

The ogre's club misses me but crushes the parked car behind me! Well, that could have been messy.

I go back into my Inventory and equip my sword. While I'm there, I check my stats and realize my Strength attribute is back to normal. Drat! I've lost the temporary strength boost from the blue gem.

Lesson learned. Instead of using it on Tank and his goons, I should have saved it for a real challenge—like right now! I just hope it's not the last lesson I'll ever learn.

"DESTROY!" he bellows as he swings his club.

I duck as his club SMASHES a lamppost behind me, sending the top half flying.

"Hey, careful with that club," I say. "I'd hate for you to accidentally smash your only brain cell." Facing a skeleton was one thing, but this guy is way more powerful. And all I've got is a measly Basic Long Sword.

"DESTROY!" he roars again.

"You know, you'd be much more interesting if you added some words to your vocabulary," I suggest. Then, I spin and—SWOOSH—slice through a police barrier. I swing again and—CLANG—he blocks my blow easily.

Then he returns the favor, swinging his club so hard it—BAM—hits me square in the back! My arms and legs flail wildly as my body CRASHES into a building!

Ugh! I'm still alive thanks to my armor, but when I look at my Health Indicator, I see:

Health	67/100

Okay, that wasn't good. I can't just attack it wildly or I'll get punished. And it's not like I have a green gem to restore my health. I need a plan. I may not be bigger or stronger than him, but I'm definitely smarter.

"KILL!" he yells, swinging his massive club.

I roll out of the way as he SMASHES a trash bin, sending garbage flying everywhere. Then, I get an idea. Since he's from the Gameverse, he doesn't know my world like I do. Maybe there's something here that can give me an advantage. I glance around for something—anything—that might give me an edge.

Bike rack?

No.

Hot dog cart?

Unlikely but I am kind of hungry.

Fire hydrant?

Hmm…

As I race toward the fire hydrant, I see something moving in the distance. Huh? What's that? Then, I realize it's a man. He's peeking out from behind a car and he's holding… a news camera?! Seriously?

"Hey, get out of here!" I yell. "It's not safe!"

But he doesn't listen.

There's something about danger that always attracts people to places they shouldn't be. Well, I can't worry about him because I've got bigger problems on my hands.

Much bigger.

I stop in front of the fire hydrant and look up to see a dangling, severed power line that's sparking with electricity. Gee, that looks dangerous.

Perfectly dangerous…

"Hey, ugly!" I shout. "Over here!"

The ogre notices me and wipes a long string of drool from its mouth. Well, that's gross.

"Catch me if you can!" I taunt.

"GRRRAAAGGGHHH!" the ogre roars as he lifts his club and rushes at me.

If I don't time this right, I'm roadkill. I wait until he's nearly on top of me, then he raises his club and I dive—

SMASH! WHOOSH!

The water from the fire hydrant spews out like a geyser, lifting the ogre straight into the air! Then, his body hits the exposed power line, and—FAZZZAAAMMM!

The ogre spasms uncontrollably, and when he THUDS to the ground his blackened, twitching body is smoldering! Holy cow! I did it!

Suddenly, a message says:

```
Enemy Vanquished:
You have gained 50 XP!
```

Followed by:

```
Congratulations! You have reached Level 2!
You can allocate +10 points across any attributes
of your choosing!
```

Yes! I leveled up! I open my Stats Window and look at my attributes which all have tiny 'up' arrows next to them along with a new box that says: 'ATTRIBUTE POINTS REMAINING: 10.'

Okay, that's cool. But where should I put them?

Well, if I'm going to be fighting monsters like ogres then I'll definitely need more Strength. So, I increase it by 5 points. I could put the rest into Agility, but if I want to level up faster I'll need more Luck to find better weapons and items. So, I put the remaining 5 points into Luck.

My stats now look like this:

MILO GARRETT		
Level: 2	XP: 75	Next Level: 150 XP
Strength: 12	Agility: 10	Stamina: 7
Intelligence: 13	Mana: 0	Luck: 10
Magic: None		
Items: Flexible Plate Armor Skin; Basic Long Sword		

Suddenly, there's a bright, white flash and the ogre is gone! In his place are two items! One is a silver bow and the other is a corked vial with a clear liquid inside of it.

Yes! The extra Luck paid off!

I pick up both items and a panel appears that says:

You have found:
1 Long Bow with Infinite Arrows (+20 Damage);
1 Vial of Holy Water!

A Long Bow with Infinite Arrows! I had this bow in Ranger Quest! What's cool is that it generates an arrow every time you draw the string. Now I can attack from long range!

But I've never seen a Vial of Holy Water before. I look at the clear liquid. It seems pretty useless.

But before I can check it out, I hear SIRENS!

The police! And if Mom is with them, I'm toast!

So, I quickly store the new items in Inventory and take off!

SEVEN

CALL ME... PIXEL MAN?

By the time I get back to my room, it's after midnight.

Luckily, Mom didn't hear me climbing up the fire escape. I crack open my bedroom door and peek into the living room, but she's not there. Whew! But then I spot a note on the refrigerator.

Whenever Mom gets called into work overnight, she leaves a note for me on the fridge. I turn on the kitchen light to read it, but all it says is that the ECPD (Empire City Police Department) needed backup for an emergency and she'd be home later. Given the disaster I just left in Central Square, I'm pretty sure I know what the emergency is.

"SNORT!"

Startled by the noise, I turn to find Ms. Rosario sleeping on the sofa. I should have known. Mom always asks Ms. Rosario to come over and keep an eye on me if she goes to work at night. Well, I'd better go back to bed. I'd hate to wake her—

"MEEOOOWWW!"

"AAAH!" I yell, jumping so high that my head nearly hits the ceiling fan!

When I turn around, I see Precious standing behind me, his tail swaying proudly.

"Bad kitty!" I whisper, my heart pumping a thousand beats a second. "You almost gave me a heart attack!"

But clearly, that's what he was going for because he HISSES at me and prances off. I look over at Ms. Rosario who is somehow still sleeping. I turn out the light and head back to my room, locking the door in case Precious is plotting a second attempt to murder me.

As I settle into bed, I stare at the Glitch Ring. Why did I have to get it first? None of this would be happening to me if I had just let ElfieMcElfFace221 have it. But no, I couldn't do that, could I?

Now look at my life.

I roll over and yawn. Boy, fighting ogres from another reality sure makes a guy tired. Then, I close my eyes and drift off...

***

Mom still isn't back when I wake up.

Ms. Rosario makes a delicious breakfast and I head off for school. Of course, the FBI is still conducting its investigation at the Third Street Station, so I have to hoof it to Eighth Street again to catch the subway. I still can't find Greylore, but I did get one surprise this morning.

Snow.

Normally, it doesn't snow this early in the year, but right now the weather is a lot like my life—unpredictable. Sadly, I'm not a big fan of the fluffy stuff. Maybe I'd feel differently if I lived in the suburbs, but for city kids like me, snow is kind of a bummer. There's nowhere to go sledding and it's no fun building a snowman out of dirty, street-plowed snow.

However, there is one benefit of snow I never considered before—gloves! And when I wear gloves, the Glitch Ring is covered. So, by the time I finally reach school, I'm feeling pretty good.

Then I run into Leon.

"Yo, have you seen Pixel Man?" he asks.

"Who?" I say.

"Pixel Man," Leon says. "You know, the crazy guy who's running around the city with a sword."

"P-Pixel Man?" I stammer.

"Yeah," he says. "That's what everyone is calling him now. It's because his body looks pixelated. I think it's his armor. You know, like in a video game. Why do you look so confused? You do know who Pixel Man is, don't you?"

I want to say, 'Of course I do. It's me, dummy!' But I can't. So instead I say, "Yeah, I think I've heard of him."

"Well, he's everywhere this morning," Leon says, looking at his phone. "Social media. TV. Everywhere. Get this, he showed up in Central Square last night and busted the whole place up."

"Busted the whole place up?" I say. "What are you talking about? He didn't do that."

"Sure he did," Leon says. "Look." Then he touches his screen and shows me his phone.

Suddenly, I'm watching a video clip of me fighting the ogre. I cringe as I see myself slice through a police barrier. How'd they even get this footage? Then, I remember the cameraman!

"Okay, I think I've seen enough," I say, gently pushing Leon's phone away. "Look, in my eyes that guy is a hero. He saved the city from an ogre."

"An ogre?" Leon says, staring at his screen. "That's what that is? Well, anyway, everyone is trying to catch Pixel Man. The mayor is offering a huge reward for any information that leads to his capture."

"What?" I say surprised. "Seriously?"

"Yeah, it's like a hundred grand," Leon says. "Imagine the gaming equipment we could buy with that!"

A hundred grand? Just to catch me?

This is getting out of hand.

"We should go for it," Leon says. "I bet we could nab him if you hit him with a dodgeball."

Okay, time to change the subject. I look up and see a blue banner hanging in the hallway. It reads:

WINTER DANCE!
FUN! GAMES! MAYBE EVEN DANCING!
FRIDAY THE 19TH @ 7:00 P.M.

"Is that new?" I ask. I don't remember seeing it before, but then again, I've only been here a few days.

"Nah, it's been up for weeks," Leon says. "It's tomorrow. I'm going. I don't play sports so my mom made me take tap dancing lessons. She said it's good for college applications. How about you? Are you gonna go?"

"Me?" I say. "Um, no. Dancing isn't my thing."

BRRRIIINNNGGG!

"That's the bell," Leon says. "I've got calculus."

"And I've got science," I say, looking at my schedule.

"Catch you later," Leon says. "Text me if you want to skip lunch to go after Pixel Man."

***

My body may be sitting here in science class, but my mind is somewhere else. I mean, I can't believe there's a reward for my capture. I'm no criminal!

That's it. I need to find Greylore ASAP! If he can get this ring off me, then no one will ever know it was—

"Mr. Garrett!"

—me? Suddenly, I hear laughter and realize everyone is staring at me, including Mrs. Klaiborne, our teacher.

"Mr. Garrett," she repeats. "Are you ready to participate now? I'm getting very tired of calling your name."

"Oh, sorry," I say.

"Thank you," Mrs. Klaiborne says. "I've been trying to explain to you that I've split the class into pairs for your lab assignment which is due tomorrow. You're partnered with Miss Donovan."

Miss Donovan? I look over at the lab tables and see all the kids paired up except for a red-haired girl wearing clear safety goggles and a big smirk. That's Claire!

"Now, if you would do us the honor of joining her at your station we can begin," Mrs. Klaiborne says.

I realize I'm the only one still sitting at a desk, so I flash an awkward smile and make my way to the lab table.

"Here's your goggles," Claire says, handing me a pair.

"Thanks," I say, putting them on.

"Why are you still wearing gloves?" Claire asks. "Maybe you didn't notice, but it's not snowing inside."

"Oh," I say, looking down at my hands. "It's kind of chilly in here." Then, I pretend to shiver and say, "Brr."

"Class, you may begin," Mrs. Klaiborne says.

I look down and see a microscope, a bottle of iodine, and some slides with labels that say: 'Onion Skin.'

Claire looks at me but I'm clueless.

"Sorry, I, um, kind of missed the assignment," I say sheepishly. "Do you know what we're doing?"

"We have to identify the cellular structure of an onion skin," Claire says as she unscrews the stopper from the iodine bottle and squeezes a drop onto a slide. "We need to draw and label all of the parts for tomorrow."

"Well, that's thrilling," I say sarcastically.

"It is for me," she says, loading a slide under the microscope. "I love this stuff."

"Oh, sorry," I say quickly. "I didn't mean to—"

"Shh," she says, peering through the microscope. "We don't want to disturb the onion skin in its natural habitat." Then, she looks at me and smiles.

I smile back. Whew, I thought I had insulted her.

"So you're not a science geek, huh?" she asks. "Do you mind prepping the next slide?"

"Um, sure," I say, grabbing the iodine bottle. "I like science, but I'm not erupting volcano models in my kitchen in my spare time."

"That's too bad," she says. "I made one yesterday. A big one too. So, what do you do for fun?"

"I like to game," I say. But as the words come out of my mouth, I realize that ever since I got stuck with the Glitch Ring, I haven't had time for gaming at all.

"My dad does too," she says.

"Really?" I say, putting a drop of iodine on the slide. "Do you ever play together?"

"With *my* dad? No," she says as she looks back into the microscope. "Gaming isn't his hobby, it's his job. He works a lot so he's never around. Slide?"

"Here you go," I say, but as I pass it over, I see a bright green glow flashing through my glove!

The Glitch Ring!

I'm so shocked I drop the slide, which CLINKS onto the table, knocking the slide cover off. I quickly hide my hand behind my back. I need to get out of here before anyone sees it.

"Are you okay?" Claire asks.

"I, um, need to use the bathroom," I say. Then, I smile awkwardly and take off. Really, Milo? Couldn't you have come up with a less embarrassing excuse than that?

"Milo?" I hear Claire call out, but I'm gone.

As I race through the hall, I look down at my right hand which is still glowing. Well, so much for trying to cover the ring with gloves. I find the nearest Boy's Room and go inside. Luckily, it's empty.

I open my Inventory Window and see the blinking globe icon. Oh, no. Not again. I take a deep breath and select it. Once again, a map of Empire City pops up with two dots. The green one is me at school, but the red one is blinking on top of a large, familiar-looking building.

The American Museum of Natural History.

I click the red dot and get:

THREE ENEMIES HAVE SPAWNED!

Three enemies? I've never seen that many before!

Suddenly, I feel torn. I want to go back to class to help Claire, but if I don't answer the call then innocent people will get hurt. But then again, there's now a reward for my capture! I don't know what to do.

But when I look at my flashing hand, I realize I don't have a choice. I've got to help.

Unfortunately, I can't just leave school because I don't have a dismissal slip. I'll have to do this the old-fashioned way. I try opening the bathroom window, but it's stuck! Great. Maybe I can pry it open with my sword.

I open my Inventory and equip my sword. But before I can try the window, I catch something moving out of the corner of my eye, and when I glance in the mirror I see someone standing behind me!

I spin around to find—

"M-Milo?" Leon says, his jaw hanging open as he stares at my sword.

I look at Leon, then at my sword, and then back at Leon. "Hey," I say casually. "So what brings you here?"

"It's the bathroom," he says. "I had to go. But is that what I think it is? Milo, you're... Pixel Man?"

"Look, it's not what you think," I say. "Please, Leon, you can't turn me in. I-I have somewhere I've got to be. People need my help."

"What do you mean?" he asks.

Suddenly, I realize that if I'm going to keep my secret identity a secret, I'll have to tell him everything. But for now, it'll have to be the short version.

"Do you remember that ultra-rare item I got from Ranger Quest?" I ask.

"Yeah," he says.

"Well, it turns out it's real," I say, taking off my glove to show him the ring. "It's this ring. It's called the Glitch Ring."

"Whoa!" he says. "It's… glowing!"

"Yeah," I say. "It gives me the ability to use items from the game, like this sword. I can also level up and increase my attributes and use special items and crazy stuff like that. That's how I was able to throw the dodgeball so hard. And now evil creatures are spawning into our world and I'm the only one who can stop them. Does that make sense?"

"Strangely, yes," Leon says. "So, you're saying that you're now like, some kind of a superhero? Like a… a boy with video game powers?"

"Exactly," I say, putting my hand on his shoulder. "So promise me you won't tell anyone or turn me in."

"Okay," he says. "I promise."

"Thanks," I say. "That means a lot."

"No problem," he says. "Hey, can I hold the sword?"

"Um, maybe later," I say as I pry open the window.

"Cool, cool," Leon says. "Well, good luck saving the world… Pixel Man."

"Thanks," I say as I climb onto the radiator and slip through the window. "Because I'm gonna need it."

EIGHT

DEMON SPAWN

Today couldn't have gone worse.

I not only abandoned Claire in science class, but now Leon knows I'm Pixel Man. And by the way, that is the worst name ever! Couldn't they have called me the Armored Avenger, or even the Noble Knight?

But 'Pixel Man?' Really?

If I survive this next encounter, I'll need to hire a PR agent. And speaking of things I'll need, I also need a faster way to get around the city. Superman can fly, Spider-Man swings on webs, and me? I'm taking the subway, which is a not-so-reliable way to save the day.

I also left my coat and backpack at school. Great.

I finally reach my stop and race up the stairs. As soon as I'm above ground, I see scores of panicked people running out of the American Museum of Natural History. Well, this must be the place.

Last year, I visited the museum with my old school. From what I remember, the building is enormous and holds over thirty-five million artifacts. But I'm not here to

see any of them. Instead, I need to find the three enemies who spawned inside. I just hope I'm not too late.

I'm about to climb the stone steps to the entrance when I hear—

"Welcome, Champion."

Huh? I spin around and see a man with bright, blue eyes and a white beard standing inside a parked taco truck. It takes me a second to reconcile his chef hat and greasy apron with his familiar smile.

"Greylore?" I say surprised. "Is that you?"

"Yes, Champion," Greylore says. "May I offer you a taco? Or perhaps a burrito?"

"Um, no," I say. "Where have you been? I've been looking all over for you. And what are you doing in this food truck?"

"I am here to provide you with the guidance you need to tackle your next quest," he says.

So, hold on. He only shows up when there's a new—

Suddenly, it hits me.

"You're an NPC!" I exclaim.

"An NPC?" Greylore says. "I am sorry but I am not familiar with that term."

"You're an NPC, a Non-Playable Character!" I say, throwing my arms in the air. "No wonder I couldn't find you. You only show up when I need to be briefed on stuff. And that skeleton fight was a tutorial so you could teach me how to use the Glitch Ring! I knew it! Now it all makes sense!"

"Champion, your reality is in great danger," Greylore says, completely ignoring my rant as NPCs typically do. "The Demons of Havoc have entered your world."

"Sorry, but did you just say 'demons?'" I ask.

"Indeed," Greylore says. "The Demons of Havoc are wicked, malevolent creatures, born in the darkest recesses of the Gameverse. Though each differs in power level, they are all formidable adversaries."

"Of course they are," I mutter.

"Infernus the Blazing Tormentor commands the fury of fire and brimstone," Greylore says. "While Glacion the Frost Reaver controls the bitter, biting cold. However, the most daunting of them all is Obsidius the Dark Assassin. He is a master of shadows, bending the very darkness to his will. These are the Demons of Havoc, and they are here for one purpose and one purpose only—to find the Three Keys of Convergence."

"The Three Keys of what?" I ask.

"The Three Keys of Convergence," he repeats. "They are magical items that can open a permanent portal between your world and the Gameverse. You must stop the Demons of Havoc before they can find them. But take note because though they are called keys, they do not resemble the kinds of keys you are familiar with."

"Then what do they look like?" I ask.

"All I am permitted to say is that you will know them when you see them," Greylore says.

Gee, isn't he helpful?

Not.

"But do not delay," Greylore continues. "Time is of the essence."

Right. As I look back at the museum, I wonder if I'm ready for this. I mean, these are demons for heaven's sake! But when I turn back to ask Greylore a few more questions, he's gone!

Darn NPC!

I guess my encounters with the skeleton and ogre were warmups. Now I've got a real quest on my hands, and if I mess it up we could be seeing a lot more of the Gameverse than anyone wants.

I realize there's no one around, so I equip my armor and explore my choice of weapons. Hmm, I think I'll try the Long Bow. I select the 2D icon, which says:

Item:	Class: Enchanted
Long Bow with Infinite Arrows	Traits: +20 Damage. Never runs out of arrows. Just pull back the string!

This was one of my favorite weapons in Ranger Quest so I'm excited to try it out in real life. I equip it and a silver bow appears in my right hand. Then, I race up the front steps to the museum.

But as I push through the door, I'm taken aback. The once majestic rotunda is a disaster. Black smoke fills the air and the smell of burnt sulfur permeates the room. The giant Barosaurus skeleton that was the centerpiece of the space is shattered into a gazillion pieces, and all of the display cases holding featured artifacts are smashed open.

I quickly scan the items scattered on the floor but I don't see a key. I sure wish Greylore would have given me more information on what the Keys of Convergence look like. Even playing the 'hot' or 'cold' game would be more useful than saying, 'You'll know it when you see it.' Especially in a place as big as this.

Now, which way should I go?

I could pick a random direction but the odds of getting lost are astronomically high. Then, I realize I may not have to guess. I pull up my Inventory and hit the globe icon. Suddenly, three red dots pop up over a map of the museum! Those are the Demons of Havoc! Well, look at that. I'm a walking GPS!

There's one on the first floor, the second floor, and the fourth floor. I'm already on the second floor and, according to this map, the demon on this floor is located in the Hall of Meteorites. So, I guess I'll go there first. Unfortunately, my map doesn't tell me which demon it is.

I sprint through the Hall of Biodiversity (is that a Dodo bird?), hang a right at the Hall of North American Forests (now that's a big tree!), and truck through the Hall of Human Origins (hello, Cro-Magnon man).

When I reach the Hall of Meteorites, black smoke fills the air and several display cases are on fire! The alarm is BLARING and the sprinklers are on, but they're not putting out the flames! I cough as smoke fills my lungs.

A demon is definitely here, and based on what Greylore told me, I'm guessing it's—

"Who dares to interfere with my search?"

—Infernus! I spin around to find the owner of the raspy voice, but I can't see him through the thick smoke.

FWOOM! Suddenly, something hot hits me square in the chest, knocking me to the ground! Then, I see:

You have been hit by: Blazing Fireball	
Health	75/100

Suddenly, a flaming figure drops in front of me! He's about my size, with red skin, tattered clothes, and two tiny, red horns on his forehead. Curiously, the water from the sprinklers isn't putting him out. I read his Stats:

INFERNUS THE BLAZING TORMENTOR		
Challenge Level: Moderate	XP: 100	
Strength: 15	Agility: 33	Stamina: 12
Intelligence: 10	Mana: 30	Luck: 5
Magic: Blazing Fireball, Smothering Smoke	Weapons: None	

He has Mana and Magic! Well, that explains where the fireball came from. If he hits me with three more of those, I'll literally be toast!

"You are either very brave," Infernus says, "or very stupid." He raises his right hand and—FWOOM—fires another Blazing Fireball!

This time, I manage to dive out of the way as it incinerates a sign behind me!

"I do not have time for this," he says. "My Smothering Smoke will finish the job. Enjoy your slow and painful death." Then, he flies into the adjoining Hall of Gems and Minerals.

But before I can follow, the Hall of Meteors suddenly fills with thick, red smoke! I try not to breathe it in, but it goes through my helmet and I start coughing like crazy. My chest feels… tight. Hard to… breathe.

Then, I see:

You have been hit by: Smothering Smoke	
Health	65/100

I've got to get out of here! So, I do what the fire safety videos teach and stop, drop, and roll my way into the Hall of Gems and Minerals. The air in this space is smoke-free and I can breathe again. Infernus has his back to me as he SMASHES through display cases and rummages through gemstones. Now is my chance!

I hold out my Long Bow and draw the string. Suddenly, a silver, glowing arrow appears out of nowhere, nocked and ready to fire! Okay, that's way cool!

I take aim and shout—

"Sorry, Flame Brain, but you're going down!"

He turns as I release the string and—THWIP—my arrow sails right over his head and—THUNK—skewers the security camera mounted on the wall behind him.

"Whoops," I say nervously as he stares at me with amusement. "I was a much better archer in the game."

"A shame," Infernus says, shaking his head. "Allow me to demonstrate what a kill shot looks like."

Before I can react—FWOOM! BOOM! I go flying, and the next thing I know—SMASH—I'm sitting inside a display case with a pile of gems on top of me! My Health Indicator pops up and says:

You have been hit by: Blazing Fireball	
Health	40/100

Ugh, that'll leave a mark. I shake off the cobwebs and scramble to my feet. He's got way more firepower than me. Then, he aims and—FWOOM—shoots again!

I dive to my right, narrowly avoiding getting fried.

Holy smokes! If I don't do something, he's gonna... gonna...

Wait a second. Holy?

"Now you will die," Infernus says.

I quickly pull up my Inventory, put away the Long Bow, and click on the Vial of Holy Water.

Item:	Class: Enchanted
Vial of Holy Water	Traits: +200 Damage to unholy creatures.

Unholy creatures? Well, if the horns fit...

I equip it and the vial appears in my hand.

"What did you say?" I ask, cupping my ear. "Sorry, that last blast hurt my hearing. Can you come closer?"

"With pleasure," Infernus says, floating toward me.

I wait until I see the yellows of his eyes. Then, I uncork the vial and douse him with Holy Water!

"AARGH!!!" he cries, his face scrunching in agony as the liquid SIZZLES against his skin. Steam is pouring off his body and he raises his arms to strike again! But then there's a bright flash and he's gone! A panel appears:

Enemy Vanquished: You have gained 100 XP!

Yes! I did it! Then, I see:

Congratulations! You have reached Level 3! You can allocate +10 Points across any attributes of your choosing!

Awesome! I see two items lying on the floor, but when I reach out to grab them, I can't move!

I'm covered in… ice? And it's so c-c-cold!
Then, this pops up:

You have been hit by: Ice Blast	
Health	15/100

Huh? Suddenly, another figure floats into the room! He looks just like Infernus, except his skin is bone white, and instead of fire, icicles are hanging from his body! I watch him land in front of a display case that houses a fist-sized, blue gem with a star-shaped pattern on top.

The Stats window over his head reads:

GLACION THE FROST REAVER		
Challenge Level: Difficult	XP: 225	
Strength: 25	Agility: 38	Stamina: 15
Intelligence: 14	Mana: 63	Luck: 10
Magic: Ice Blast, Snow Storm	Weapons: None	

Glacion! I swallow hard. I barely survived fighting one demon, and now I have to deal with another! And this one looks way stronger!

"Infernus, you fool," he says, looking at the big, blue gem. "I bet it was here all along."

Here? What was here?

Glacion SHATTERS the glass and I read the sign hanging over the display case, which says: SECRET STAR SAPPHIRE. ORIGIN UNKNOWN.

As Glacion picks up the gem, a panel appears:

Item:	Class: Unknown
Secret	Traits: This item
Star Sapphire	contains high levels
	of Mana

Hang on. That's no ordinary sapphire. It has Mana! I guess that's what Greylore meant. Mana is how I can tell what the Keys of Convergence are!

I have to get it from Glacion. But I still can't move!

Then, Glacion wheels on me. "You destroyed my brother," he says as cold vapor escapes from his lips, "and now I will destroy you." Then, he raises his hands.

No! If he hits me one more time, I'll die for real!

"BROTHER!" comes a deep voice from nowhere.

Suddenly, Glacion's expression turns from anger to fear. "Y-Yes, Brother!" he answers.

Brother?

"HAVE YOU FOUND THE KEY?" the mysterious voice asks.

"Y-Yes!" Glacion says. "I have found it, Obsidius!"

Obsidius? That creepy voice belongs to Obsidius?

"But Infernus—" Glacion starts.

"HIS FATE IS OF NO CONSEQUENCE," Obsidius interjects. "ONLY THE MASTER MATTERS. NOW COME TO ME AT ONCE, BROTHER. WE DO NOT WANT TO DISAPPOINT NIKADEMOS."

Nikademos? There's that name again.

"Of course, Brother," Glacion says. Then, he looks at me and says, "Next time you will not be so lucky."

As he flies away, I breathe a sigh of relief. That was close. And now that he's gone, the ice starts melting.

I tense my muscles and push until the ice barrier cracks. I'm still alive but I feel like a failure. The demons have one of the Keys of Convergence, and I need to stop them before they find the other two. Then, I see the items Infernus dropped on the floor.

As I pick them up, a panel appears:

You have found:
1 Dragonhide Flight Armor Skin (+20 Defense);
1 Flaming Long Sword (+50 Attack)!

Whoa! These are major upgrades! I need to keep boosting my Luck attribute so I can find more cool stuff.

But before I can check them out, I hear a MEEP!

That's my phone! Maybe Mom is looking for me.

I drop my armor and the new items into my Inventory and pull my phone out of my pocket. When I look at my text messages, I see:

<Hey, Milo! Leon gave me your number. He said you had a dentist appointment you forgot about. Do you want to stop by my place to finish our science project? It's due tomorrow. We can even make a volcano (jk). P.S. I also have your backpack. Claire.>

NINE

HOUSE OF CHAOS

I know I shouldn't be going to Claire's place right now.

But the way I see it, there are two ways I could suffer an untimely death. The first is if the Demons of Havoc destroy me for trying to stop them from getting the Keys of Convergence. The second is when Mom kills me for flunking out of Empire City Magnet School. And since I have no clue when I'll deal with the first scenario again, I figure I should at least try to avoid the second.

As I walk to Claire's apartment, I process everything that happened at the museum. Even though I eliminated Infernus, Glacion got away with one of the Keys of Convergence. That's not good, but at least I now know what I'm looking for. That star sapphire had Mana. So, I just need to find two other objects that have Mana too.

Of course, that's easier said than done because I won't know where the other two keys are located until I get an alert from the Glitch Ring. I pinch the ring through my glove. Why was I trusted with this responsibility? I'm no hero. I'm just a kid who's good at gaming.

As I turn onto 5th Avenue, I think back to how Glacion cowered like a puppy when he heard his brother's voice. But I have to admit, Obsidius did sound intimidating. I'm just lucky I got out of there alive. And I also managed to avoid the police.

Before leaving the museum, I stored all my stuff in Inventory so I'd look like a normal kid. Thankfully, I didn't run into Mom because I would have had a hard time explaining why I wasn't in school.

Suddenly, I realize that I've reached Claire's address. I look up at the beautiful high-rise building with awe. Wow, you've got to be super wealthy to live here. But then again, I shouldn't be surprised since she takes a limo to school.

"May I help you?" the doorman asks. He's wearing a crisp, blue uniform with bright, gold buttons and a cap.

"Um, yes," I say, straightening my hoodie. "I'm here to see Claire Donovan. She, um, invited me."

"Mr. Garrett, I presume?" he says, opening the gold-plated door to the building. "Miss Donovan is expecting you in the penthouse. If you would kindly remove the snow from your shoes and then proceed to the elevator."

"Oh, sure," I say, stomping my shoes on the mat.

I enter the lobby and walk across the polished marble floor. There's fancy furniture and beautiful paintings on the walls. The shimmering chandelier alone is probably worth more than my entire apartment building. I push the elevator button, and when it arrives I get inside and hit the 'P' button for the penthouse. I've never been in a penthouse before so this should be interesting.

As the elevator ascends to the fiftieth floor, I practice my greeting. "Why, hello, Claire, it is wonderful to see you." No, too formal. "Good afternoon, Claire, you're looking well." Definitely no. "Yo, Claire. What's up?"

Just then, I catch my reflection in the mirrored wall and gasp. Uh oh, I look far from penthouse-ready. There's a hole in my hoodie and my hair is standing up like a porcupine. I try pushing it down but it won't stay.

Great, this isn't what I—

BING!

Huh? How'd I get there so fast? Suddenly, the elevator doors spring open and, instead of seeing Claire, I'm staring at a bald, mustached man wearing a tuxedo!

"Good afternoon, Mr. Garrett," the man says with a very formal-sounding English accent. "I am Barnaby, the Donovan's butler." I'm about to check his stats when he says, "No coat in this weather? How unwise. May I take your gloves?"

"What?" I say. "Oh no. I'm good, thanks."

"This way then," he says, his eyebrows arching. "Miss Donovan is waiting for you in the game room."

The game room? As he leads me through the apartment, I peer into the spacious rooms. Each one is perfectly decorated and I suddenly feel awkward being here. I mean, I usually forget to make my bed!

Just then, Barnaby opens a sliding door and says, "Miss Donovan, your guest has arrived."

My jaw drops. The game room is three times bigger than my entire apartment! To my right is a massive gaming setup with multiple VR glasses, giant monitors, and the coolest-looking gaming chairs I've ever seen. In the center of the room are a pool table, a foosball table, and a ping pong table. And lining the wall to my left is a series of classic, stand-up arcade games. It's like I died and went to heaven.

"Hey, Milo," Claire says, waving at me from the pool table. "I'm over here."

"Oh, hey," I say, stepping into the room. "Sorry, it's just, well, wow."

"Yeah, I get it," she says, shrugging her shoulders.

"Miss Donovan, please ring if you need me," Barnaby says. Then, he looks at me suspiciously and closes the door.

"Lovely chap," I say.

"He means well," Claire says. "So, any cavities?"

"Cavities?" I say confused. Then, I remember Leon covered for me by telling her I went to the dentist. "Oh, no. Flossing, that's the key to excellent dental hygiene."

"Thanks for the tip," she says.

Flossing? Seriously, Milo?

"I probably already know the answer," Claire says, "but you can take your gloves off if you want."

"Um, no, that's okay," I say. "I run cold."

Now would be the perfect time to change the subject. "Listen, I'm really sorry for skipping out on you in class today. Thanks for giving me a chance to finish the project."

"Sure," she says, picking up a pool cue. "I finished it in class. But since we're lab partners I thought you might want to check it over before I turn it in. It's on the table next to you."

"Cool," I say, picking up the worksheet to review it. She put both of our names on it and answered every question with perfect penmanship. "It looks good to me. Who knew that onions were the philosophers of the vegetable world? They have more layers than people."

"Ha," she says as she lines up a pool shot and—SMACK—sinks a ball into the corner pocket.

"Nice shot," I say. "It must be amazing to live here."

"Sometimes," she says. "The truth is that I'm usually on my own. My mom is always busy with her social engagements and charity work, and my dad is a workaholic. Barnaby isn't much fun either."

"You don't say?" I offer in my best English accent.

"Ha!" she snorts.

Just then, I notice a bunch of award plaques on the wall. I lean in for a closer look at one, which reads:

GAME OF THE YEAR:
RANGER QUEST BY CHAOS GAMES

Huh?

And the award plaque next to it says:

GAME DEVELOPER OF THE CENTURY:
LORD CHAOS

Suddenly, everything clicks.

"Um, Claire?" I say. "You said your dad worked in the gaming industry, right?"

"Yeah," she says, lining up another shot. "He's kind of famous. His real name is Sterling Donovan, but everyone knows him as—"

"—Lord Chaos?" I say, finishing her sentence.

"Yeah, how'd you..." she says, rising to see me staring at his award. "Ah, have you heard of him?"

Heard of him? I want to tell her that I worship him but I don't want to come across like a stalker. So, I simply say, "Um, yeah. Ranger Quest was my favorite game."

"A lot of people loved it," she says. "Then something weird happened and my dad can't get it working again. He's been pretty stressed out lately."

So something really did happen to the game. And if Lord Chaos can't fix it, no one can. Then, I get a strange thought. Did I break it when I got the Glitch Ring?

There's a small display case on the table with a gold coin inside of it. Looking closer, I realize it's not a coin, but an old-fashioned game token. There's a sign in front of the case that reads:

THE FIRST TOKEN USED TO PLAY THE
VERY FIRST ARCADE GAME CREATED
BY LORD CHAOS.

That's cool. Then, a transparent window appears above it. But before I can read it—KNOCK! KNOCK!

The knocking at the door startles me and I turn.

"Oh, that must be Barnaby," Claire says.

But when the door slides open, it's not Barnaby, but a tall, fit-looking man with messy, reddish-gray hair. He's wearing a stained button-down shirt and an old pair of jeans. He's holding a Styrofoam coffee cup and there are dark circles under his eyes, like he's been awake for days.

"Dad!" Claire exclaims. "I didn't know you were home. What are you doing here?"

Dad? That's Lord Chaos? I'm in shock. He's never made any public appearances before so no one knows what he looks like. But now he's actually here, standing right in front of me! Except, he doesn't look anything like I expected. I quickly read the Stats over his head:

Sterling Donovan		Level: 1	
Strength: 10	Agility: 11		Stamina: 11
Intelligence: 35	Mana: 0		Luck: 0
Magic: None		Items: None	

"I left some papers in my office," he says. Then, he notices me and says, "Oh, hello there."

"Dad, this is Milo," Claire says. "He goes to my school. Milo, this is my dad."

"Hello, Milo," he says with a warm smile.

"Um, hi," I say softly, very much starstruck.

Suddenly, it dawns on me that he might know something about the Glitch Ring. After all, it came from his game! But I can't ask him in front of Claire.

"Milo knows who you are," Claire says quickly. "He plays Ranger Quest. Well, at least he used to."

"I'm so sorry," her dad says. "I honestly don't know what happened. I've been working day and night to get it running again, but no luck yet."

"That's okay," I say. "I'm sure you'll figure it out."

"I hope so," he says, "because the gamer forums are roasting me alive." Then, he looks down at my hands and asks, "Are you cold? I can have Barnaby turn up the heat so you can take off your gloves."

"Oh, that's okay," I say, looking at my gloved hands. "I think one of my parents is half-lizard."

"Okay," he says with a chuckle. "Well, it was nice to meet you, Milo. Oh, can you do me a favor?"

Wow. Lord Chaos is asking me for a favor?

"Um, sure," I say.

"Don't tell anyone my secret identity," he says with a wink. "I like my privacy, especially for Claire's sake."

"Oh, of course," I say. "I would never…"

"Great," he says. Then, he smiles at Claire and says, "I'll see you later, dear."

"Bye, Dad," Claire says.

As I watch him leave, I realize I have a million questions that aren't going to get answered.

"Do you want to play pool?" Claire asks.

"Um, sure," I say. But then—

MEEP! That's my phone! I pull it out and find a text:

<Ms. Rosario: Milo, are you okay? Where are you? Can you pick up a chicken on your way home?>

Oh no! With everything going on, I completely forgot to tell Ms. Rosario where I was. I quickly text her that I'm fine and on my way home.

"On second thought," I say, "I should probably get going. I've got to get home before dinner."

"Oh, okay," Claire says, looking disappointed. "Let me walk you out."

"Thanks," I say, following her back to the elevator.

She presses the button and we both smile but don't say anything.

"Well, thanks again," I say.

"Wait, your backpack!" she says. She disappears for a few seconds and then comes back with my bag. "I put your coat inside."

"Thanks," I say, taking it from her. "I guess I couldn't ditch my homework if I tried."

"Ha," she says with a smile.

Suddenly, the elevator doors open and I step inside. As I turn to say goodbye, the doors start to close and she blocks them with her foot.

[85]

"Are you going to the dance tomorrow night?" she asks.

"The dance?" I say. With everything going on, I forgot all about it. "Um, no. I wasn't planning on it."

"Too bad," she says. "It should be fun."

"Well, then I guess I'll be there," I say with a smile.

"Great," she says, smiling back.

"Great," I say.

"See you in school tomorrow," she says, removing her foot from the elevator.

"Yeah," I say. "See you in—"

But the doors slam shut before I can finish my sentence.

TEN

WE GOT ROBBED

My subway ride home is a long one.

I'd love to check out the items I got at the museum, but I don't want to freak out the other passengers. I'm really curious about the Dragonhide Armor because it wasn't in the game. But that'll have to wait until I complete my next quest—bringing Ms. Rosario a chicken.

The one thing I can do, however, is allocate the attribute points I got from defeating Infernus. I pull up my Stats window and add +1 to Strength, +1 to Agility, +3 to Luck, and +5 to Mana because, well, why not?

Now my Stats look like this:

MILO GARRETT		
Level: 3	XP: 175	Next Level: 250 XP
Strength: 13	Agility: 11	Stamina: 7
Intelligence: 13	Mana: 5	Luck: 13
Magic: None		
Items: Flexible Plate Armor Skin; Basic Long Sword; Long Bow with Infinite Arrows; Dragonhide Flight Armor Skin; Flaming Long Sword		

Not bad, aside from all the 'unlucky' 13s.

By the time I reach Sal's Corner Grocery Store, it's dark outside. I grab a whole chicken from the refrigerator section and head to the register. But when I reach the counter, Sal doesn't notice me because he's watching the TV mounted on the wall. The news is on, and a female reporter is at the American Museum of Natural History!

"…another appearance from the mysterious person known as Pixel Man," the reporter says. "Police have released footage from inside the museum showing Pixel Man damaging museum property. Let's take a look."

What? I didn't damage museum property!

Just then, a grainy, black-and-white image of me appears on the screen. I'm standing in the Hall of Gems and Minerals in full body armor but there's no sign of Infernus. Then, I watch myself aim my Long Bow and fire. The arrow flies straight toward the camera and then everything glitches and goes black!

"As you just saw," the reporter continues, "Pixel Man disabled the security camera. Then, he went on to destroy several wings of the museum, damaging hundreds of irreplaceable artifacts. Strangely, after a full audit of the museum, it was determined that only one item was missing—the Secret Star Sapphire." Then, they cut to an image of the large, blue gemstone. "It's called the Secret Star Sapphire because no one knows where it came from. As the story goes, it was simply left in a cardboard box that the museum staff found years ago. Nevertheless, valued at over one million dollars, this artifact was clearly Pixel Man's target all along."

Wait, what? That's not true—that's not even what happened! Glacion took the star sapphire, not me!

"Hey, Milo," Sal says, noticing me for the first time. He mutes the volume with the remote control and scans my chicken. "How about that? Pixel Man is a thief."

"Oh, I don't know about that," I say, my voice rising as I pay him for the chicken. "I think he's just... misunderstood."

"Misunderstood?" Sal says, looking at me strangely as he bags the chicken. "Stealing a million dollar gemstone isn't a misunderstanding, it's a crime. Here's your chicken. Say hello to Ms. Rosario for me."

I nod and smile, but I'm only smiling on the outside. On the inside, I feel sick to my stomach. No one knows what's really happening and the whole city is against me.

As I walk to my building, I cover my head with my hood. Even though no one knows I'm Pixel Man, I'm starting to feel paranoid. I mean, it's only a matter of time until the FBI figures out my true identity.

When I reach my building, I race up the stairs to my floor. I just want to relax at Ms. Rosario's until Mom comes home. But as I head for her apartment, I notice something unusual.

The door to my apartment is ajar.

That's odd.

I mean, I left this morning before Ms. Rosario, but she wouldn't forget to close our door. After all, she takes safety more seriously than anyone. Getting into her apartment is like getting into Fort Knox! And Mom wouldn't leave the door open either. I put down the grocery bag and listen for any noises, but there's nothing.

I consider getting Ms. Rosario but change my mind. After all, I don't want to put her in danger. So, I grab the doorknob and push open the door.

As it CREAKS open, I notice the lights are off. I stand there for a few seconds but still don't hear anything. Hmm, I guess I could be wrong. Maybe Mom did come back for something and forgot to close the door. So, I reach inside and flick on the lights. Then, I gasp.

The place looks like it was hit by a hurricane. Chairs are knocked over, drawers are emptied, and papers are strewn about everywhere. Our TV is smashed on the floor and our couch cushions have been slashed.

I-I can't believe it. We've been robbed!

Mom! My instincts take over and I run through the living room to her bedroom. Luckily, she's not here, but her room has been ransacked too. Then, I open the door to my room and my heart sinks.

My stuff is scattered everywhere. Birthday cards I saved from Mom, art projects I did as a kid, pictures of Mom and me. All ruined. The only good news is that my gaming computer is at—

Holy cow! Ms. Rosario!

I race into the hallway, pick up the grocery bag, and knock frantically on her door.

"Ms. Rosario?" I shout. "Are you in there? Are you okay? Ms. Rosario?"

Seconds later, I hear the familiar sound of bolts unlocking and breathe a sigh of relief. Ms. Rosario opens the door and I give her a big hug.

"Hola, Milo," she says with a confused expression on her face. "I'm happy to see you too."

Precious stares at me from the back of the couch and I'm surprisingly happy to see him too.

"Y-You don't understand," I say, nearly out of breath. "Our apartment was robbed. Didn't you hear anything?"

"No," she says, her eyes wide. "But I was cooking so the TV was on loud."

Just then, I hear the TV blaring in the background. It's all in Spanish, except for the words "Pixel Man."

"We have to call the police," I say. "We've got to call Mom. Oh, here's your chicken."

"Of course, of course," she says, taking the bag. "Come inside, mi Milo."

As she calls my mom, I collapse on the couch and feel my heart beating fast. On TV, I see the same footage of me in the museum, except this time it's being reported in Spanish. I grab the remote control before Precious can spear me with his claws and turn it off.

***

"What do you mean nothing was stolen?" I ask.

It's late and Mom and I are in Ms. Rosario's spare bedroom. Mom is still on duty and I realize it must be weird for her to be investigating a break-in at her own apartment.

"I mean exactly what I said. Nothing was taken," Mom says. "I checked everything. My computer, our birth certificates, my bank checks. They're all still there. I don't understand why someone would break into our apartment and not take anything."

"Yeah," I say, scratching my chin. "Neither do I."

"Anyway," she says, "we're still looking for fingerprints or anything that will lead us to who did it. But right now it looks like a pretty clean job. Whoever did it is clearly a professional."

"Wonderful," I say sarcastically.

"Listen, Milo," she says, "I want you to stay with Ms. Rosario tonight. Our team won't be finished for a few more hours and you have school tomorrow."

"I can't go to school!" I say. "Not after this."

"Yes you can," Mom says. "It'll help take your mind off things. I know it's not easy but try to get some sleep."

"Fine," I say reluctantly. "I'll try."

"Remember, it's just stuff," she says. "The only thing that matters is that we're both safe. I love you."

"I love you too," I say.

"Now get some sleep," she says.

Then, she hugs me and leaves.

"Don't worry," Ms. Rosario says as she comes in to hug me. "Precioso and I will protect you."

"Thanks, Ms. Rosario," I say, hugging her back. "I guess I'll try to get some sleep."

"Buenas noches, Milo," she says. Then, she turns off the light and closes the door.

I lie down but sleep is the last thing on my mind. Whoever trashed our place clearly didn't want money, electronics, or files. So what did they want?

I look at the Glitch Ring. Could they have been looking for this? Suddenly, the ring starts glowing!

No, not again. Not now. I open my Inventory and mentally press the blinking globe icon. A map of Empire City pops up and I see two dots. The green dot is me, but the red dot is blinking over a large building in midtown.

The Empire City Public Library!

I click the red dot and get:

TWO ENEMIES HAVE SPAWNED!

I sit up. Two enemies! That's got to be them—the Demons of Havoc! Another Key of Convergence must be at the Empire City Public Library!

I've got to stop them, but this time I could use some help. I grab my phone and text Leon. I sure hope he's up.

<ME: Leon, I need your help!>

A few seconds later, I get:

<LEON: Yo, I'm not fencing your sapphire.>

<ME: I didn't steal the Secret Star Sapphire! The demons did! I need your help.>

<LEON: You want my help? Does that mean I'm like, your sidekick? And did you say 'demons???!!!'>

<ME: Yes, I'll explain later but can you get a list of all the artifacts in the Empire City Public Library?>

<LEON: Do ducks waddle? Of course I can! Oh, and call me Pixel Kid!>

<ME: What?>

<LEON: Well, if you're Pixel Man, then I'll be Pixel Kid. I know, cool right? But you can't have it. The name is mine. Trademark pending.>

<ME: Just call me when you've got the list.>

<LEON: Will do. Pixel Kid, out!>

Okay, that was probably a huge mistake. But if Leon can help me find what I should be looking for, then maybe I can nab the next Key of Convergence before the demons do. Unfortunately, that means I need to escape from my building first. The problem is that it's currently crawling with cops. I think my only way out is down the fire escape. So, I go to my window, open it up, and—

"MEEOOOWWWW!"

"AAUGH!" BAM!

"Ow!" I say, rubbing my noggin. And when I look up, Precious is staring at me from the fire escape! Crazy cat. I was so startled I hit my head on the bottom of the window. I forgot that Ms. Rosario lets him out at night.

"Bad kitty," I whisper as I climb out the window. "Now don't tell any—"

"MEROWL!" he cries out.

Great. If I don't get out of here, I'm gonna get caught. I just wish I had a faster way to get to—

Wait, maybe I do!

I open my Inventory Window and see an armor icon with wings on it. Yes! I select it and see:

Item:	Class: Enchanted
Dragonhide Flight Armor Skin	Traits: +20 Defense. This armor gives you the power to fly. Just flap away!

Enchanted armor that lets me fly?

Awesomesauce!

As I equip it, Precious jumps back and I can see why. I'm not only decked out in light, green-scaled armor, but I also have two giant wings sticking out of my back!

This is incredible! I'm super excited to try it out!

"Don't be jealous, Precious," I say casually. "Only cool cats like me get to fly. Smell ya later."

Then, I step off the fire escape and plunge to my doom.

ELEVEN

READING ROOM RUMBLE

It's funny what flashes through your mind when you're falling to your death.

I think about how mad Mom will be when she learns I was Pixel Man. I think about Leon who will be bummed that he never got to be my sidekick. There's Claire who will be disappointed I never made it to the dance. The demons will open a portal to the Gameverse and take over the world. And then there's Precious, who's about to have the time of his life watching me splatter on the pavement.

What a way to die. I thought my Dragonhide Flight Armor Skin would fly on its own, but now I remember the description said, "Just flap away." Duh! Dragons can't fly unless they flap their wings, so I need to do the same!

I concentrate hard on flapping, and suddenly I hear a RUSTLING noise as my wings extend and start beating! Then—FWOOSH—I've righted myself and I'm soaring into the air! Holy dragons, I did it!

Sorry to ruin your night, Precious.

As I climb higher and higher, I can actually see into the windows of skyscrapers! Whoops, sorry ma'am.

Okay, enough of that. I've got to get to the Empire City Public Library, but this steering thing is a wee bit tricky. Whoa, here comes a building! Flap, Milo, flap! I gain more air and my toes just scrape the roofline.

Whew, that was close! I quickly figure out how to turn by angling my wings and rolling my body, and soon I'm flying like a pro. I have to say, gliding over the city is incredible! From up here, cars look like toys and trees look like broccoli. You know, maybe the Glitch Ring isn't all bad. Especially if it lets me do this. Plus, I'll never have to take the subway again!

I pull up my map, zero in on the library's location, and—BRRRIIINNNGGG! BRRRIIINNNGGG!

Huh? That's my phone! It's ringing inside my pants pocket. I can't get it now, but maybe there's another way. I pull up my Inventory Window and see a blinking phone icon. Wait, do I have Bluetooth?

I mentally click it and say, "Hello?"

"Yo, Pixel Man," Leon says. "I've got the list."

"You rock, Leon!" I say.

"That's Byte Boy," Leon says. "B-Y-T-E, get it?"

"What?" I say. "What happened to Pixel Kid?"

"Nah, I figured I should do my own thing," Leon says. "You know, have my own superhero swagger."

"Whatever," I say, rolling my eyes. "Just look for an object on that list that might have a high level of Mana."

"Okay, but there are thousands of artifacts at the Empire City Public Library," Leon says. "Did you know they have Thomas Jefferson's handwritten copy of the Declaration of Independence?"

"Leon, focus," I say. "We need to figure out what might be a Key of Convergence."

"That's Byte Boy, remember?" Leon says. "We should stick to our official codenames. You never know who might be listening."

"Fine, Byte Boy it is," I say, exasperated. "Can you please look at the list now?"

"This list is huge," Leon says. "We need a clue, something to help us narrow it down. Tell me, do you remember anything unusual about the star sapphire?"

Now that's a great question. Then, I remember what the sign said above its display case!

"Leon, I've got it!" I exclaim.

"Byte Boy," he says.

"Byte Boy," I say, holding my tongue. "Is there anything on that list that says something like, 'Origin Unknown?'"

"Origin Unknown?" Leon repeats. "Hold on, let me run a search query."

I hear Leon typing as I approach midtown. The library is just a few blocks away.

"Yes!" he says suddenly. "There's one item here that says, 'Unknown Origin,' which is just the reverse of 'Origin Unknown.'"

"Great, what is it and where is it?" I ask.

"It's a book called 'The Future of Coding Virtual Worlds,'" Leon says. "According to this, it's old, maybe from the 1970s and before modern video games. It says that no one knows where it came from and there's no author listed. It's located somewhere on the third floor."

"Great work!" I say. "Thanks, Leon!"

"It's not Leon," he says. "It's Byte B—"

CLICK! Oops, was he still talking? Sorry, Byte Boy.

Suddenly, my destination comes into view. It's a massive, white building that looks more like a Greek temple than a library. Six large columns flank the front doors and several robed figures are carved into its façade. Two lion statues stand guard at the base of a wide stairway that leads up to the entrance.

It's nighttime so the library is closed, but clearly the demons didn't care because they blew the doors right off their hinges. I tuck in my wings, fly through the entrance, and glide up the stairwell to the third floor. When I reach the landing, I exit into a rectangular room that has an impressive painting of Prometheus, the God of Fire, on the ceiling. It's cool, but I'm not here to sightsee.

CRASH!

That came from nearby! I peer through the archway on my right and see upended tables, broken lamps, and scattered books. Drat, they got to this floor first.

None of the books in this area have Mana so I've got to keep looking. I open my Inventory, equip my Long

Bow, and fly into the next room where I find more of the same.

SMASH! That was even closer!

I hug the wall, peek into the adjoining space, and gasp in shock. It's an enormous reading room that runs two city blocks long and nearly fifty feet high! Murals are painted on the ceiling, arched windows frame the walls, and fancy chandeliers hang overhead. Wooden tables with little green lamps fill the room for as far as the eye can see, and the shelves are packed with thousands of books!

Wonderful. The one book I need isn't going to be easy to find. But then again, maybe that's a blessing in disguise because Glacion is already here, and he's yanking every book off the shelf looking for it!

Sorry, Glacion, but your library card is about to be revoked! I draw back the string of my Long Bow and an arrow appears. Then, I yell, "Freeze, foul demon!"

That was a huge mistake, because before I can fire my arrow, Glacion wheels around, and—UGH! I-I can't move! Not again!

You have been hit by:	
Ice Blast	
Health	75/100

"That will put you on ice until I find the artifact," Glacion says as he turns back to the bookshelves. "Then I will finish you once and for all."

Why did I open my big mouth? I try pushing my way out of the ice but I can't! And it's getting c-c-colder!

As I watch Glacion grab book after book, I realize that maybe the demons can't see which items have Mana like I can. Maybe they can only sense it through touch, which is why they have to handle every single item. That's an advantage for me, so maybe I should use it.

Although my body is frozen, I can still move my eyes. I glance around the room. scanning every shelf I can see, but there's nothing. Then, I spot a display case in the distance under a large sign that says: BOOKS ABOUT CODING.

Coding? I scan the books in the display case until I land on a worn-looking book with a blue cover.

Then, this pops up:

Item:	Class: Unknown
The Future of Coding Virtual Worlds	Traits: This item contains high levels of Mana

That's it! That's the Key of Convergence! And Glacion is just a few feet away! I've got to get out of this ice prison so I can get to it first.

But I can't. I'm frozen in place! Or am I?

Glacion may have trapped me physically, but he didn't trap me mentally, and I'm pretty sure I've got the perfect item to melt my way out of this mess. I open my

Inventory and find what I'm looking for—the Flaming Long Sword! I click on it and get this:

Item:	Class: Uncommon
Flaming Long Sword	Traits: +50 Attack. Can produce ongoing burn damage.

Perfect! I put away the Long Bow and equip the Flaming Long Sword. The next thing I know, I'm gripping a golden hilt in my right hand and a long, flaming blade is poking out of the ice! The heat is so intense the ice starts melting immediately.

But Glacion is getting closer to the book. C'mon, sword, hurry up! Suddenly, I'm able to move my right arm, then my right leg, and then my whole body!

I'm free! Whew, the heat coming off this sword is so intense I need to be careful not to grill, I mean, kill myself. Uh oh! Glacion is almost there!

I flap my wings and take to the air. Glacion has his back to me and I'm coming in hot!

When I'm only a few feet away, I raise my sword and shout, "Surprise!" I swing down but Glacion evades my strike and my blade slices through a bookshelf like a hot knife through butter!

Note to self: Stop talking before you attack!

"Very well," he says with a wicked grin. "I have not yet found the Key, but I will gladly end your life."

Before I can react, he raises both hands and I'm suddenly flying in an indoor blizzard! A blustery wind howls as heavy snow falls and the temperature drops below f-f-freezing! Then, this appears:

You have been hit by: Snow Storm	
Health	65/100

Great. And what's worse is that my flaming sword is fizzling out! I try flapping my wings to gain higher ground, but they're covered in ice and I start sinking!

You have been hit by: Snow Storm	
Health	55/100

This b-b-blizzard is draining my health! I have to stop G-G-Glacion, but I'm going down and my sword is almost out! I need a p-p-plan!

You have been hit by: Snow Storm	
Health	45/100

I look at my extinguished sword and a lightbulb goes off. I don't know if this will work, but I'm only going to get one shot at this so I'll need to time it perfectly.

I pull up my Inventory Window and put away the Flaming Long Sword, shielding it from the blizzard. Then, as my feet touch the ground, I focus on one last flap, pushing off the ground with all of my might! Icicles fly from my wings as I head straight for Glacion!

The demon's eyes go wide. "What are you—"

This time, I manage to keep my mouth shut as I re-equip my Flaming Long Sword which is now blazing strong again like new!

Yes! It worked!

"NO!" Glacion shouts.

But it's too late because I swing and—FWOOM—slash him down! The blizzard stops as he CRASHES into a table. I follow him down, striking him again and again with the Flaming Long Sword. Suddenly, there's a bright, white flash and this appears:

Enemy Vanquished:
You have gained 225 XP!

Followed by:

Congratulations! You have reached Level 4!
You can allocate +10 Points across any attributes
of your choosing!

Wow, I jumped another level! Then, I see this:

```
Congratulations!
You have learned the Spell:
Lightning Strike (10 points Mana)
```

Wait, what? I've finally got Magic!

Then, an item appears where Glacion was lying! It's a bottle with a skull and crossbones emblem. I pick it up and this pops up:

```
You have found:
1 Poison Antidote!
```

That could be useful, but I need to grab the—

CRASH!

Startled, I spin to see a shadowy tendril breaking through the display case and wrapping itself around the book! Where did that come from? Then, I remember what Greylore said and a chill runs down my spine.

"YOU MAY HAVE DEFEATED MY BROTHERS, CHILD," comes a deep, rumbling voice. "BUT I AM FAR STRONGER."

Suddenly, a panel appears above the tendril.

OBSIDIUS THE DARK ASSASSIN		
Challenge Level: Extreme	XP: 400	
Strength: 38	Agility: 77	Stamina: 35
Intelligence: 21	Mana: 85	Luck: 16
Magic: Shadow Touch; Dark Dread; Soul Cleaver	Weapons: None	

My stomach sinks.

Does his Challenge Level say "Extreme?"

Well, scared or not, I've got to get that book away from him! But before I can move, the room goes pitch dark, so dark it even swallows the light coming from my Flaming Long Sword!

I-I can't see a thing!

"THIS IS YOUR LAST WARNING," Obsidius says, his voice echoing through the chamber. "IF YOU CHOOSE TO INTERFERE AGAIN, I WILL DESTROY YOU."

Then, the darkness lifts and Obsidius and the book are gone!

TWELVE

DISASTER AT THE DANCE

"**Y**ou look so handsome," Mom says.

"Mom, please," I say. But as I check myself out in the mirror, I have to admit I clean up pretty well.

Tonight is the school dance and I'm dressed to impress. My hair is slicked back and I'm wearing a burgundy sports coat with a blue, button-down shirt and brown khakis. But despite how good I look, I don't feel great about going.

After all, Obsidius now has two of the three Keys of Convergence. Instead of dancing, I should be out trying to find him. But I told Claire I'd be at the dance so I need to keep my word.

Luckily, Mom was able to put our apartment back together after the break-in. Of course, the fact that nothing was stolen still makes me nervous. If the intruder didn't take anything, then what were they looking for?

"Are you sure you want to wear that ring to the dance?" Mom asks. "It clashes with your outfit."

I look at the Glitch Ring and feel guilty.

A part of me just wants to tell her about everything—Greylore, the Gameverse, Pixel Man.

But instead, I say—

"That's okay. It's kind of my good luck charm."

Falser words have never been spoken.

"Okay," she says. Then, she looks at the clock and says, "We'd better get going or you'll be late."

I follow her into the kitchen where she grabs her coat, purse, and keys. I put on my coat and gloves and we head outside to her police cruiser. It's no limo, but it'll do. Besides, if we get stuck in traffic, I'll beg Mom to turn on the sirens.

After slogging our way across town, we're nearly at school when a bulletin comes over the police radio:

"Attention all units, attention all units," comes a man's voice. "Please stay on high alert for the individual known as 'Pixel Man.' The suspect is classified as armed and extremely dangerous. I repeat, armed and extremely dangerous. Exercise caution when approaching. In addition, the Chief of Police has authorized the use of necessary force to neutralize any threats."

I swallow hard and look over at Mom, who is listening closely to the bulletin.

"Um, just out of curiosity," I say, "what exactly does 'necessary force' mean?"

"It means that we're authorized to do whatever it takes to stop Pixel Man," she says, looking at me with a steely gaze. "And that includes shooting to kill."

"Shooting to kill?" I say, slumping down in my seat.

"That's right," she says. Then, she flashes a big smile and says, "Now get ready to boogie because we're here!"

As we pull up to the curb, I see lots of nicely dressed kids heading into school. Well, this is it. I hope nothing goes wrong tonight. Please let nothing go wrong tonight.

"Have fun and text me when you need a ride home," Mom says as she straightens my collar. "Oh, and Milo, don't get into any trouble."

"Who, me?" I say as I get out of the car.

"Very funny," she says. Then, she looks at me with a goofy smile and says, "My baby is so grown up."

"Goodbye, Mom," I say as I shut the door.

As Mom drives away, I hear—

"Yo, Milo!"

I turn to see Leon running toward me. He's wearing a dark green suit, a lime green shirt, and a bright green bow tie. "So, what do you think of the threads?" he asks as he spins around.

"I think you look like a walking pickle," I say.

"Says the guy who runs around in a pixelated suit," Leon says. Then, he puts his hand in front of his mouth and whispers, "Any news on the demon dude?"

"Nothing yet," I say. "Hey, have you seen Claire?"

"Claire?" Leon repeats, his left eyebrow arching. "Does someone have a crush?"

"Um, no," I say quickly, my face feeling flush. "I just promised her I'd be here. Come on, maybe she's inside."

We enter the school and I hang up my coat on the coat rack. I consider taking off my gloves but think better of it. Then, we head to the gym where we run into Mr. Stanley and a bunch of adult chaperones.

"Boys," Mr. Stanley says with a nod. "No funny business tonight."

"Oh, you don't have to worry about that," Leon says. "My friend here doesn't have a funny bone in his body."

We step into the gym which has been completely transformed. The lights are dimmed, decorations are hanging from the rafters, and a DJ is blasting music so loud the floor is vibrating. The girls have taken over the dance floor and the boys are clustered near the punch bowl, trying—and failing—to look cool.

I don't see Claire anywhere.

"I'm gonna walk around for a minute," I say to Leon. I stroll around the gym but still can't find her.

Suddenly, the music stops and the gym goes pitch dark. As the crowd moans, Mr. Stanley calls out, "Everyone stay calm. We probably just tripped the circuit breaker. Give us a minute to fix it."

Great. Even if Claire was here, I couldn't see her.

Just then, a firm hand lands on my shoulder and a gruff voice says, "Hey, Garrett, want some punch?"

"Tank?" I say. "Is that—"

POW!

Oof! Tank punches me in the stomach so hard that I drop to my knees.

"That's for the dodgeball game," he says.

Suddenly, the lights turn back on and the music starts thumping again. I try to stand but I can't, and when I look up, I see Tank smiling and high-fiving his two buddies who are walking back into the gym. That's when it hits me. That power outage was no accident, it was a setup so Tank could deck me without being seen!

"Milo, are you okay?" comes a familiar voice.

Claire!

I try to get up but I'm in so much pain I can't. Well, this certainly isn't the impression I was hoping to make.

"Here, let me help you," she says as she takes my arm and helps me to my feet.

"Thanks," I say, finally catching my breath. But when I look at her, it's taken away again. Her hair is up and she's wearing a shiny green dress. She looks glamorous.

"Milo, what happened?" she asks.

"I, um, had too much punch," I say quickly. "But I'm okay now. You, um, look nice."

"Thanks," she says smiling. "You too."

"Oh, thanks," I say, wiping my forehead. "I looked better before the flop sweat."

Just then, a glint of gold catches my eye from something hanging around her neck. It's her necklace. It looks like a round pendant hanging on a gold chain. But when I look closer, I realize it's not just any pendant, but the game token I saw in her game room!

Suddenly, a panel appears above it that says:

Item:	Class: Unknown
Arcade Game Token	Traits: This item contains high levels of Mana

My jaw drops.

The game token! It's the last Key of Convergence!

"You noticed," she says proudly, touching the token. "I saw you admiring it so I asked my dad if I could turn it into a necklace. Thankfully, he said yes. It's the first token he used to play the very first arcade game he ever created. Do you like it?"

"No!" I blurt out and she looks shocked. "I mean, I like it, but…"

Suddenly, I notice a faint green glow. I look down and my ring is flashing through my glove. Oh no.

"What's that?" Claire asks, looking down.

But I don't answer. Instead, I open my Inventory Window and hit the globe icon.

"Hey, Claire," Leon says, walking over with a cup of punch. "Nice dress. Love the color. Did he say you looked like a pickle too?"

I see two dots on the map, one green and one red.

And they're both right on top of the school!

"Milo, are you okay?" Leon asks.

"No," I say wide-eyed. "Listen, we've got to—"

RIIIPPP!!!

Suddenly, the gym's roof is torn off!

As kids SCREAM and race for the exits, I look up and see a dark, shadowy cloud hovering over us, blocking out the night sky.

I-I can't believe it! It's Obsidius!

But before I can get Claire's necklace away from her, a thick, black tendril wraps around her waist and lifts her high into the air.

"Milo!" she calls out. "Help!"

"Claire!" I shout.

That's it! I don't care if everyone sees me turn into Pixel Man, I've got to help her!

But then I hear—

"Milo!"

It's Leon! He's frozen in place as a chunk of the roof is falling right over his head! Instinctively, I dive on top of him, equipping my Flexible Plate Armor Skin and—

THOOM!

The debris lands hard on my back and I see a window that says:

Health	95/100

"Leon, are you okay?" I ask.

"Y-Yeah, I-I'm good," Leon says from beneath me.

I push off the debris and help Leon to his feet. By now, the entire gym is empty and Claire is gone!

"I'm so sorry, man," Leon says.

"I'm just glad you're okay," I say. "But now I've got to find Claire."

"Can you track her?" he asks.

"No," I say, "but I think I can track him." I pull up my map and see his red dot crossing the city. "I'm going after them." I pull up my Inventory and replace my Flexible Plate Armor Skin with my Dragonhide Flight Armor Skin.

"Whoa, now those are some cool threads," Leon says, admiring me. "What do you want me to do?"

"Find a computer," I say. "I'll call you soon."

"Roger that," Leon says. "Good luck, Pixel Man."

"Thanks, Byte Boy," I say, taking off into the air.

"Oh, I forgot to tell you!" I hear him call out. "I changed my name again! I'm now going by—"

But I don't hear the rest, because I'm long gone.

THIRTEEN

A GLITCH IN THE SYSTEM

I can't catch a break.

Ever since I got the Glitch Ring, my life has been one disaster after another. I mean, even something as innocent as a school dance has turned into a catastrophe! But then again, I never expected Claire's necklace to be one of the Keys of Convergence.

Now she's been kidnapped by Obsidius and I'm the only one who can save her. And that's not all. Obsidius has all three Keys of Convergence, which means that he can open a portal to the Gameverse!

At least I can track him on my map. I've been flying after him, following him to the west side of Empire City. There aren't any skyscrapers out here, so I'm probably visible from the ground. But at this point, I don't care who sees me. I just need to find Claire and stop this crazy demon before it's too late!

I pull up my Stats to remind myself where I allocated the attribute points I earned from defeating Glacion.

MILO GARRETT		
Level: 4	XP: 400	Next Level: 450 XP
Strength: 14	Agility: 12	Stamina: 8
Intelligence: 13	Mana: 10	Luck: 15
Magic: Lightning Strike (10 pts)		
Items: Flexible Plate Armor Skin, Basic Long Sword; Long Bow with Infinite Arrows; Dragonhide Flight Armor Skin; Flaming Long Sword; Poison Antidote		

That's right, I added +1 to Strength, +1 to Agility, +1 to Stamina, +2 to Luck, and +5 to Mana to try out my new Lightning Strike spell. One day I'd love to raise my Intelligence which would probably solve a whole bunch of problems in my life.

I check the map to discover that the red dot— otherwise known as Obsidius—has stopped at a building along the river. It's not a building I recognize, so I decide to dial "L" for help. I open my Inventory, click the phone icon, and say, "Call Leon." The phone rings once, and—

"Code Crusher here, over," Leon says.

"Code Crusher?" I say.

"That's my new name," Leon says. "It rocks, right?"

"Um, if you say so," I say. "Look, I need your help. I'm flying over a building at 213 Riverside Boulevard. I need to know who owns it."

"You're on Riverside Boulevard?" Leon says. "There's an awesome game shop on that street but my mom won't ever let me—"

"Not now, Leon," I say. "Just give me the info."

"It's Code Crusher," he says. "Hang on." I hear him typing in the background, and then he says, "It's a warehouse. Let me see if I can find out who owns it." There's more typing, followed by, "Oh, wow."

"Oh, wow?" I repeat. "Oh, wow, what?"

But before he can answer, I hear—

"Young man, what are you doing in here?"

"Uh oh," Leon says.

"Who is that?" I ask. "Leon, where are you?"

"I'm still at school," Leon says.

"Please log off that computer," the voice says. It sounds like a man's voice.

"The cops are everywhere," Leon says, "but I managed to sneak into the computer lab. I've gotta go, but the building is owned by Chaos Games. Code Crusher, out!"

Chaos Games?

"Young man, get off that—"

CLICK! And he's gone.

My mind is spinning. Chaos Games is Claire's dad's company. Why is Obsidius taking Claire there?

I don't know the answer but I plan to find out. I avoid the floodlights and touch down on the far side of the warehouse. I need to get inside, but all the doors are closed and the windows are boarded up.

Clearly, someone is hiding something in there.

I sprint around back and spot the loading dock where trucks unload cargo. Except, there aren't any trucks here. The only vehicle I see is a Rolls Royce. That's weird. I run up the ramp and test the back door. Yes, it's unlocked! I tuck in the wings of my Dragonhide Armor and quietly slip inside.

The warehouse is filled with wooden crates stacked one on top of the other. As I walk by, I notice each crate is stickered with this address and the words: CHAOS GAMES. Suddenly, I hear—

"Let my daughter go," comes a familiar voice.

I freeze. 'My daughter?' That's Claire's dad! And that Rolls Royce must be his car!

"I THINK NOT," rumbles another familiar voice.

Obsidius!

I can't see anything from this position, so I stay low and make my way closer. I duck behind another stack of crates and peer around the corner.

Then, my heart skips a beat.

Claire's limp body is hovering in the air, being held aloft by a dark, nebulous cloud! Her chest is moving up and down which means she's still breathing. Thank goodness for that.

Well, the black cloud holding her is clearly Obsidius, and he's floating in front of Claire's dad who has his back turned to me. Strangely, Mr. Donovan is wearing a black suit with a long, red cape. Why is he dressed like that?

But that's not the only strange thing I see because standing between them is a twenty-foot-tall, iron triangle. Each corner of the triangle has a receptacle, and the

Secret Star Sapphire is in the one on the lower left while the book from the library is in the one on the lower right!

The top receptacle is empty, and Claire is still wearing the game token necklace around her neck!

I think back to what Greylore told me. If the demons get all three Keys of Convergence, they'll open a permanent portal to the Gameverse. Well, this triangle must have something to do with creating the portal, so I need to stop Obsidius before he can use it!

I equip my Long Bow and draw back the string. An arrow appears nocked and ready to fire, but I realize it's a bad idea. After all, I can't hit Obsidius when he's a cloud. Plus, what if I miss and hurt Claire?

I need to get Claire away from him. But how?

"I'm warning you, demon," Mr. Donovan says, pointing at Obsidius. "Release her or you'll be sorry."

That's it! If I team up with Claire's dad, then I can take on Obsidius while he gets Claire to safety. Of course, my plan is missing a few important details—like, for instance, how I'll actually defeat Obsidius. But then I look at my arrow and get an idea. It's risky but it might work.

"Don't worry, Mr. Donovan," I say, stepping out from my hiding spot. "Pixel Man is here." Then, I aim my Long Bow at Obsidius and say, "Listen up, demon. This is a magic arrow that disperses clouds, so I suggest you give him the girl before I vaporize you."

But Obsidius doesn't fall for my bluff. Instead, he just laughs at me.

"You think that's funny, huh?" I say. "Well, you won't be laughing when I fire this arrow up your—"

"Don't do anything rash, Milo," Mr. Donovan says. "Just give me the ring and I'll take care of him myself."

I freeze.

Um, did he just call me Milo? But... my face is covered by my helmet, so how did he know it's me? And even more importantly, how did he know about the ring?

"Hand it over, Milo," he continues, holding out his hand. "I know it's you under that armor. And please, don't call me Mr. Donovan. I'm Lord Chaos now."

"I-I don't understand," I say confused as I keep my bow aimed at Obsidius. "How did you know it's me?"

"I created Ranger Quest, remember?" he says. "I've been searching for the user known as 'TheMightyMilo#1' ever since he got the Glitch Ring. But before I could find him, the game shut down and all user accounts were deleted, including his profile and IP address. Then, by coincidence, a mysterious hero called 'Pixel Man' shows up with all of the abilities from my game. I knew he was the one who found the Glitch Ring, but I still didn't know who he was. That is, until I met you."

As he steps toward me, I take a step back.

"You're the real life Mighty Milo," he continues. "Your name matched the user name who acquired the Glitch Ring. And when you wouldn't take your gloves off in our apartment, well, that's when I knew."

I swallow hard. But then I realize something.

"You raided my apartment!" I exclaim. "You were looking for the ring!"

"Guilty as charged," Lord Chaos says with a devious smile. "Although it was Barnaby, not me. He's much better at doing the dirty work. But he couldn't find it."

Of course he couldn't. I can't take it off my finger!

"That's why I had to lure you here," he continues.

"Lure me?" I say confused. "What do you mean?"

"Oh, it was simple," Lord Chaos says. "I knew that if Claire was in trouble, you would do anything to save her. So, we staged this kidnapping to bring you here, away from the public eye. And you took the bait."

As I process what he just said, I glance up at Claire who is still unconscious and being held by Obsidius.

"Are you saying you put your own daughter in harm's way... just to get to me?" I ask. "You're sick!"

"I prefer to call myself ambitious," he says, his smile twisting into something much more sinister. "You see, I'll do anything to get what I want. And that ring you're wearing was supposed to be mine."

"What are you talking about?" I ask.

"You only have it because of an error. A glitch, if you will," he says. "That ring was always meant for me. You probably don't even know how it got here, do you?"

"I-I got it from the game," I say.

"Yes," Lord Chaos says. "But that's not the whole story. You see, the ring comes from an alternate reality called the Gameverse."

His words hit me like a bolt of lightning. For some reason, I always thought the ring just came from the game. It never occurred to me that it could have come from the Gameverse itself!

"It's true," he continues. "You see, one night when I was working on Ranger Quest, something unusual happened. I had been coding all night and I was tired, but when I finally stopped typing, the code kept going, as if it were writing itself. For a moment, I thought I had lost my mind. But then I realized it wasn't game code that was being written, but rather a message written in code. It wasn't easy to decipher, but eventually I translated it, only to discover that it was written by someone from another reality called the Gameverse. He called himself Nikademos."

Nikademos! There's that name again!

"He said that he was trapped in a prison he could not escape from," Lord Chaos continues, "and he needed my help to break free. If I promised to bring him here, to my reality, then he would use the game to send me a ring of great power—a ring that would allow me to rule over my world. Once I fulfilled our bargain and Nikademos was by my side, he would show me how to unlock the ring's full potential. Of course, I'm no fool. I only accepted his proposal after he swore his allegiance to me. Then, he sent his most trusted agents to help me find three magical items that were hidden in our reality—the Keys of Convergence. With the Keys of Convergence and the power of the ring, I could then open a portal that would bridge our two realities, setting Nikademos free."

"Are you insane?" I shout. "You made a pact with a monster! But why? You had everything anyone could ever ask for—money, fame, a daughter who loves you."

"That may be enough for ordinary people," Lord Chaos says, "but I am far from ordinary. Sure, I could go on making the rules for virtual, make-believe worlds. But now I actually had the chance to rule over a real one! With Nikademos' help, I could reshape this planet and the people who live on it in any way I desired! All I needed was the ring I was promised. Except things didn't go according to plan. When Nikademos sent the ring through the game, a glitch in the code prevented me from obtaining it. Instead, the ring was programmed to be retrieved by the game's greatest player, and congratulations, that player was you. But now that I've finally found you, I want my ring. So hand it over and no one will get hurt."

I-I can't believe it! Lord Chaos, my idol, is evil!

"I couldn't give you the ring even if I wanted to," I say. "It won't come off my finger."

"No worries," Lord Chaos says, pulling out a knife. "I have just the solution for that."

FOURTEEN

BOSS BATTLE

My mind is reeling.

Claire's dad, also known as Lord Chaos, made a pact with Nikademos to take over the world! This entire time he's been working behind the scenes, helping the Demons of Havoc collect the Keys of Convergence so they can open a portal to the Gameverse to bring Nikademos here!

But that's not all. Once Claire's dad discovered my true identity, he kidnapped his own daughter to lure me to his warehouse! All so he could claim the one thing he needed to carry out his devious plan.

The Glitch Ring.

Except, it's stuck on my finger and won't come off.

"If you can't remove the ring," Lord Chaos says, holding up his knife, "I'll be happy to do it for you."

I swallow hard and glance at Claire. She's still unconscious and being "held" by the black cloud known as Obsidius. I'd like to think her dad wouldn't hurt her, but now I'm not so sure.

"TAKE THE RING, HUMAN," Obsidius bellows. "I AM GROWING IMPATIENT."

Well, that seals it. Even if her dad wouldn't harm her, Obsidius definitely would! I can't let anything happen to Claire. I need to get her away from him.

"Okay, everyone just stay calm," I say. "I'll give you the ring, but first you need to put Claire down."

"YOU ARE IN NO POSITION TO NEGOTIATE TERMS, CHILD," Obsidius says.

"No, it's okay," Lord Chaos says, looking at me with wild eyes. "Put her down, Obsidius. Gently."

At first, the shadow cloud swirls in objection, but then he carefully lowers Claire to the ground.

"Now move away from her," I say.

"Go on, Obsidius," Lord Chaos says, watching me closely. "Do as he says."

Obsidius hesitates, then flows away from her body.

"Now the ring," Lord Chaos demands.

Great, now what? If he gets the ring, he'll use it to activate a portal to the Gameverse. I can't give it to him, and I certainly don't want him to cut off my finger to get it. I still can't believe this is happening. I still can't believe he set me... up?

That's it! This might be a bad move, but I've got to try. I open my Inventory Window and put away my Long Bow and armor. Pixel Man is gone and now it's just me, Milo, unarmed and flying by the seat of my pants.

"Let me do it," I say, looking into Lord Chaos' eyes.

"Do what?" he says. "What are you talking about?"

"I'm talking about opening the portal," I say, making a fist with my ring hand. "Let me be the one who opens the portal. Look, you said things didn't go as planned the last time you worked with Nikademos. You said there was a 'glitch' in the code that prevented you from getting the ring, right? Well, what if it wasn't a glitch? What if Nikademos was setting you up to fail all along? And if so, who knows what's going to happen when you open the portal? If something goes wrong, wouldn't you rather have it happen to me than you?"

Lord Chaos shoots Obsidius a suspicious look and then looks back at me. Clearly, he's thinking about it.

"Very well," he says finally. "I'll let you open the portal. But when you're done, I'll get that ring one way or another. Now, stand inside the triangle."

As I follow his instructions, I realize this probably isn't the best idea, but at least it keeps the ring away from him. Lord Chaos kneels beside Claire and removes her game token necklace. Then, he holds it up to Obsidius who swirls around it and carries it to the triangle's uppermost receptacle.

"Now, Milo, raise your right hand so the ring is in the center of the triangle," Lord Chaos commands.

I swallow hard. Now is my chance to stop this, but when I look back at Claire, Obsidius is hovering over her.

I-I don't know what to do.

"Raise the ring!" Lord Chaos shouts.

I raise my right hand and, to my surprise, the Glitch Ring suddenly sparks with green electricity! Then, three beams of green light shoot out from the ring, connecting to each corner of the triangle! The ring—it's linking up with the three Keys of Convergence!

Just then, green beams of light fire out from each Key of Convergence, meeting at a spot ten feet in front of me, forming a small, green circle in mid-air! Then, the small, green circle begins to swirl and grow, expanding in diameter—two feet, and then four feet, and then six feet!

Okay, clearly this was a big mistake. I've got to stop it, but I can't lower my arm! The beams coming from the Glitch Ring have locked it in place!

"Keep going!" Lord Chaos shouts as he moves behind me.

"*YESSS!!!*" comes a distant voice that sounds like a raspy whisper. "*WIDER! OPEN IT WIDER!*"

"FATHER!" Obsidius calls out. "COME, FATHER! WE ARE WAITING FOR YOU!"

Father? Nikademos is his father?

Suddenly, the green portal turns black, like there's a hole hanging in mid-air, and I see tiny lights twinkling inside. Are those stars? Is that the Gameverse?

"*WIDER STILL!*" comes the voice again, but this time from closer. Much, much closer.

Then, I gasp as four gigantic, red fingers with pure black fingernails appear and hook onto the edge of the portal, stretching it downward!

The hairs on the back of my neck stand on end as I realize those are Nikademos' fingers, and they must be two feet long each!

"YES, FATHER!" Obsidius exclaims with glee.

Then, a Stats window appears:

NIKADEMOS		
Challenge Level: Unknown	XP: Unknown	
Strength: Unknown	Agility: Unknown	Stamina: Unknown
Intelligence: Unknown	Mana: Unknown	Luck: Unknown
Magic: Unknown	Weapons: Unknown	

That's weird. Why is everything "Unknown?"

Okay, Milo, you can't worry about that now. You've got to stop this before it's too late! I try pulling my right arm down with my other hand but it won't budge!

"R-Remember, Nikademos," Lord Chaos stammers, clearly stunned by the size of his ally. "We had a deal. I freed you from your prison so you must serve me."

"FOOL! I WAS NEVER IMPRISONED," Nikademos says as his other hand grips the top of the portal. *"YOU WERE BUT A PAWN, AND ONCE I ENTER YOUR WORLD YOU WILL SUFFER THE SAME FATE AS ALL OF THE OTHERS!"*

"N-No…" I hear Lord Chaos whisper from behind me. And then he calls out, "Milo, close the portal!"

"I'm trying but… I can't!" I yell.

"YOU WILL DO NO SUCH THING," Obsidius

says, swirling over Claire's body. "OPEN IT WIDER!"

Okay, I'm definitely NOT doing that. I look up at the Glitch Ring. If I can't move it out of the way, then maybe I can shut off its power!

I mentally try to turn off the ring but it's not working. I pull up my Inventory Window and look for an On/Off button but can't find one! I need to try something else!

I quickly flip through my items. Long Sword. No. Long Bow. No. Flaming Sword. Nope. Dragonhide Flight Armor Skin. Dragonhide Flight Armor… Skin?

I look up at my bare right hand. Hmm.

I don't know if this will work, but it's worth a shot.

I equip the Dragonhide Flight Armor Skin which immediately covers my entire body, including the Glitch Ring on my right hand! Suddenly, the beams from the ring to the Keys of Convergence stop flowing!

Yes! Covering the ring cut the power supply!

"NO!" Nikademos shouts.

Then, I notice the beams from the Keys of Convergence are weakening and the portal is shrinking!

"FATHER!" Obsidius cries out.

"YOU WILL PAY FOR THIS!" Nikademos yells. Then, with one desperate lunge, he reaches through the portal with a giant hand!

I flap my wings hard and soar over his outstretched hand as it grabs Lord Chaos instead!

"NO!" Lord Chaos shouts as Nikademos pulls him

back through the portal before it vanishes into thin air!

I'm in shock. Just like that, Nikademos and Lord Chaos are gone!

"FATHER!" Obsidius cries. Then, he swirls around me and says, "CHILD, I WILL DESTROY YOU!"

Uh oh, someone got left behind! I wish I could have planned that better so Obsidius got dragged through the portal too, but it's too late now. I need to go into flight mode to draw him away from Claire.

"Catch me if you can!" I shout. I spy Claire's necklace and grab it out of the receptacle. Then, I soar through the warehouse to get as far away from her as possible. When I reach the other side of the building, I touch down on a catwalk and equip my Long Bow.

Then, I hear—

"I AM OBSIDIUS THE DARK ASSASSIN," comes a rumbling voice from all around. "I AM THE DARKNESS. I AM THE SHADOW. I AM YOUR DOOM!"

Suddenly, dark tendrils spring out from all sides! I fire my bow at one but the arrow just passes right through! Great, new plan needed! I take off again as a tendril swipes at me and misses, but another solidifies and—OOF!—punches me so hard I CRASH into a crate!

Then, I see this:

You have been hit by:
Shadow Touch

Health	70/100

I manage to flap my wings and go airborne again, but I know I'm in trouble. After all, how do you fight a shadow demon?

"YOU WILL NOT SURVIVE THIS ENCOUNTER," Obsidius bellows. "AND AFTER YOUR DEMISE, I WILL CLAIM THE GLITCH RING FROM YOUR LIFELESS BODY AND REOPEN THE PORTAL MYSELF."

"Not if I can help it!" I shout bravely.

"SADLY, YOU CANNOT," he answers.

Just then, the entire warehouse goes dark!

W-What happened to the lights? And why is my whole body q-q-quivering? BUMP! What was that noise?

Then, I see:

You have been hit by:	
Dark Dread	
Health	55/100

Dark Dread? W-What's that? And why is my heart racing so fast? Then, I realize it's not me but his Magic.

He's making me afraid of the dark!

WHAM!

Just then, something hits me hard in the back and I go flying end over end until I SMASH into another crate!

I feel… dizzy. Then, this pops up:

You have been hit by:	
Shadow Touch	
Health	30/100

This isn't fair! How can I fight if I can't see? And now I'm down to just 30 points of health! If he hits me two more times I'm a goner!

Suddenly, something wraps around my leg, lifts me into the air, and—SMASH—slams me face-first into the wall! I drop to the ground.

You have been hit by:	
Shadow Touch	
Health	5/100

Feel... weak. Can't... get up. Need... health. I pull up my Inventory but I don't have any healing gems.

"WE HAVE REACHED THE END," Obsidius says, and when I look up, he's hovering over me.

N-No! I try to get up, but... I can't.

"NOW YOU WILL FEEL THE AGONY OF MY GREATEST POWER—SOUL CLEAVER!" Obsidius thunders. "AS YOU FEEL YOUR VERY SOUL SPLIT APART, I ADVISE YOU TO STEP TOWARD THE LIGHT, FOR IT WILL BE THE LAST THING YOU EVER SEE."

Light? Holy cow, I almost forgot!

I open my Inventory and navigate to the Spells grid. It used to be empty, but now there's an icon of a hand shooting a lightning bolt in the first box!

I click on it and see:

Spell:	Mana Points: 10
Lightning Strike	Traits: +100 Attack. Fires a bolt of pure lightning at any target.

Why didn't I think of it earlier?

The only way to fight darkness is with light!

I equip the spell as Obsidius whirls around me! I still can't see anything, and even if I could, I wouldn't have a solid target to aim for. I sure wish Greylore was here because I've never used Magic before and I'm not exactly sure how to do this!

"IT IS TIME TO DIE!" Obsidius says.

Instinctively, I close my eyes, raise the Glitch Ring into the air, and shout, "LIGHTNING STRIKE!"

A warm sensation shoots through my right hand, and—FATHWOOM—pure electricity fires out in every direction, bathing the warehouse in blinding light!

"AAARRRGGHHH!" I hear Obsidius scream.

I shield my eyes, and when I open them again the darkness is gone! Then, I hear WHIMPERING.

I turn and see a small creature lying helplessly on the floor, electricity crackling all over its body.

It's Obsidius! He looks just like Infernus and Glacion, but he's way smaller and has char black skin. That's when I realize that he's been hiding his true form inside his shadows all along. He may have sounded intimidating, but he's really just a runt!

"N-No..." he says breathlessly as he sees me approaching. "P-Please... M-Mercy..."

I equip my Flaming Long Sword.

"Mercy?" I say. "Like you were going to give to me? Or to Claire? I don't think so."

I strike him multiple times with my Flaming Sword.

There's another bright, white flash, and then:

Enemy Vanquished:
You have gained 400 XP!

Followed by:

Congratulations! You have reached Level 6!
You can allocate +20 Points across any attributes
of your choosing!

Whoa! I jumped two whole levels!

But that's not all because two items appear where Obsidius was lying! There's a round, iron shield and something that looks like a small, pointy stick. I pick them up and see:

You have found:
1 Iron Shield (+25 Defense);
1 Parasite Wand!

That shield would have come in handy a few seconds ago, but I've never heard of a Parasite Wand before. I wonder what that does.

Then, out of the corner of my eye, I see something gleaming on the floor. It's Claire's necklace! I must have dropped it during the battle. I scoop it up and see:

Item:	Class: Unknown
Arcade Game Token	Traits: This item contains high levels of Mana

It still has Mana. If I don't get rid of it, then someone might use it to reopen the portal. But I'd hate to destroy the game token. It means so much to Claire.

I look down at the Parasite Wand. Hmm...

I drop it into Inventory and it becomes a 2D icon. Then, I select it and read:

Item:	Class: Enchanted
Parasite Wand	Traits: Drains Mana from any object. This is a single use item.

Whoa! That gives me an idea!

I store the shield in Inventory and take off. When I reach Claire, I'm relieved to see she's breathing, but she's still unconscious. I decide not to move her in case she's hurt and place a call for help. I open my Inventory and hit the phone icon. It rings once and then—

"Milo?!" comes Leon's excited voice. "I mean, Pixel Man, are you okay?"

"Yeah," I say, "but Claire needs an ambulance."

"Is she okay?" Leon asks.

"I think so," I say. But as I look at her face, I wonder how she'll feel when she finds out about her dad.

"I'll call for one right away," he says. "But you should get out of there before they show up."

"I'll wait until the ambulance arrives," I say. "Besides, I've got something I need to do."

"Okay," he says, "but don't get caught."

"Don't worry," I say. "I won't."

I hang up with Leon and gather the artifacts, placing the game token, book, and star sapphire next to one another.

Then, I equip the Parasite Wand and take aim.

EPILOGUE

PRESS START

I can't believe it's over.

It's been a week since the warehouse battle and I'm still recovering. I wish I could forget about it, but I can't because I relive it every night in my dreams. Except these dreams are nightmares where Nikademos breaks through the portal and destroys me.

Needless to say, I feel lucky things turned out the way they did. But more importantly, I'm relieved that I won't ever have to be Pixel Man again.

At the warehouse, I used the Parasite Wand to drain all of the Mana from the Keys of Convergence. No more Keys means no more portal. And no more portal means that my job as Pixel Man is done.

Before help arrived, I put Claire's necklace back around her neck. Once she was in the care of the paramedics, I snuck out and returned the star sapphire to the museum and the book to the library. I also included a personal note from Pixel Man to clear my name.

That should be the end of it.

Of course, Mr. Donovan's disappearance is still all over the news. There's a big reward for anyone with information on his whereabouts, but it'll never be collected. No one will find him where he went.

I visited Claire at the hospital a few days ago. She's doing fine physically but is struggling emotionally with everything that's happened. I feel bad. Part of me wants to tell her the truth, but I can't. After all, it would crush her to know that her dad was not only responsible for her kidnapping but that he also wanted to conquer the world.

For now, I'm just happy to get my life back to normal. I'm meeting Leon for ice cream at that allergy-friendly place he keeps talking about. I don't know how good allergy-free ice cream will taste, but it's the least I can do for the guy after everything he's done for me. But this time, I'll take the subway.

"Remember, Milo," Mom says as I walk into the kitchen, "we have big plans for pizza and a movie tonight. Don't be late."

"Don't worry," I say. "I'll be home on time."

"Great," she says, "And remember to——"

"——look out for Pixel Man," I say. "I remember but you saw the news. He returned both of those artifacts and left a note saying that he didn't steal anything."

"Sure, but I don't believe him," she says. "That stuff was so hot he probably couldn't sell it. Now they think he was involved in the school and warehouse incidents too. It wouldn't shock me if he turns up again soon."

"Oh, I wouldn't worry about it," I say. "I doubt we'll be seeing him again."

"Oh, really?" she says. "And why not?"

Whoops. "Um, because no one has seen him for days," I say, putting on my coat. "Maybe he retired."

"Maybe," she says, "but I doubt it. One day he'll slip up and—BAM!" She slaps the table hard like she's squashing a bug. "Anyway, have a good time. I love you."

"Um, love you too," I say. I exit into the hall where I find Ms. Rosario carrying two bags of groceries. "Let me help you with that," I say, taking a bag.

"Gracias, Milo," she says. "Where are you going?"

"For ice cream," I say as she unlocks her door. When she opens it, Precious pops his head out.

"Have fun," she says, taking the bag back.

"I will," I say. "Later, Ms. Rosario." Then, I look down at Precious and nod.

"MEERROWWLL!" he says, nodding back. Maybe I'm wrong, but I think that was a meow of respect.

I race down the stairs and head outside. It's still cold out so I stuff my hands in my pockets to keep them warm. As I walk, I rub the Glitch Ring with my thumb.

When I first got it, I thought it was the worst thing ever. But after learning what Mr. Donovan—or rather, Lord Chaos—would have done with it if he had gotten it instead, I'm glad it was me.

As I turn onto Third Street, I hear music. Out of the corner of my eye, I see a guy playing guitar and an open guitar case on the ground for tips. Without breaking stride, I pull a quarter out of my pocket and toss it into the case. Then, I hear—

"Good afternoon, Champion."

I stop and look at the bearded guitar player.

"Greylore?" I say. "Is that you?"

"Congratulations, Champion," he says, his blue eyes twinkling. "You stopped the Demons of Havoc and prevented the portal to the Gameverse from opening."

"Yeah, about that," I say. "You forgot to tell me about Nikademos. He's kind of a big deal, you know? Like, literally."

"My apologies, Champion," Greylore says. "On your journey, there will be things I am permitted to tell you and things that you must discover for yourself."

"On my journey?" I say confused. "Hang on, are you saying this isn't over?"

"Over?" Greylore says with a broad smile. "The Gameverse is home to many beings of great power who will seek to conquer your world."

Suddenly, I feel like I'm gonna puke.

"So, you're saying I'll never be able to take this ring off?" I ask. "That I'll be Pixel Man forever?"

"You are the Champion," Greylore says, "the fate of your world is in your hands."

Yeah, I'm definitely gonna puke.

MEEP! That's my phone.

"Hold on," I say, and when I look down I see a text:

<LEON: Yo, where are you? They have the craziest flavors here like avocado banana crunch! Oh, I also made a list of 103 new codenames I want to run by you. We can go over the pros and cons of each when you get here. So, when are you getting here?>

Oh no. Anyway, back to business.

"Listen, Greylore, I don't—"

But he's gone! AHH! Why does he keep doing that?

Well, as much as I want my life to be normal again, I guess it's just not in the cards. Pulling up my Stats, I review the attributes I upgraded after defeating Obsidius:

MILO GARRETT		
Level: 6	XP: 800	Next Level: 1,050 XP
Strength: 15	Agility: 14	Stamina: 10
Intelligence: 13	Mana: 20	Luck: 20
Magic: Lightning Strike (10 points)		
Items: Flexible Plate Armor Skin, Basic Long Sword; Long Bow with Infinite Arrows; Dragonhide Flight Armor Skin; Flaming Long Sword; Poison Antidote; Iron Shield		

Not too shabby. I take a deep breath and look at my right hand. Well, Glitch Ring, I hope you're ready because more bad guys from the Gameverse are coming, and when they do, Pixel Man will be right here to stop them!

The adventure continues in
The Boy with Video Game Powers 2!

Order Your Copy Today!

YOU CAN MAKE A BIG DIFFERENCE

Calling all Champions! I need your help to get The Boy With Video Game Powers in front of more readers.

Reviews are extremely helpful in getting attention for my books. I wish I had the marketing muscle of the major publishers, but instead, I have something far more valuable, loyal readers, just like you! Your generosity in providing an honest review will help bring this book to the attention of more readers.

So, if you enjoyed this book, I would be very grateful if you could spare a minute to leave a review on the book's Amazon page.

Thanks for your support!

R.L. Ullman

DON'T MISS THE BOY WITH VIDEO GAME POWERS 2!

To Milo's surprise, he must rescue a princess from the Gameverse. However, evil forces in the Gameverse don't want the princess to escape, and they'll do whatever it takes to stop him. But as Milo is about to learn, this princess is no damsel in distress, and rescuing her just might be the biggest mistake he'll ever make!

Order Your Copy Today!

MILO'S LEVEL UP CHART

XP Required per Level:

LEVEL	XP	LEVEL	XP
1	0	6	650
2	50	7	1,050
3	150	8	1,450
4	250	9	2,250
5	450	10	3,050

As the Champion's Level Increases, the XP Value of Enemies Increases:

CHAMPION'S LEVEL	ENEMY CHALLENGE LEVELS: XP VALUES			
	EASY	MEDIUM	DIFFICULT	EXTREME
1	25	50	75	100
2	50	100	150	200
3	75	150	225	300
4	100	200	300	400
5	125	250	375	500
6	150	300	450	600
7	175	350	525	700
8	200	400	600	800
9	225	450	675	900
10	250	500	750	1,000

DISCOVER YOUR NEXT FAVORITE SERIES BY R.L. ULLMAN

EPIC ZERO Series:

Growing Up in a Superhero Family is Cool, Unless You're Powerless...

Elliott's parents are superheroes. His sister is a superhero. Heck, even his dog is a superhero. But Elliott is a "Zero," which is super-speak for powerless. When Elliott is the only one left to save the day, will he find the power to be an epic hero—or will he always be an Epic Zero?

MONSTER PROBLEMS Series:

Half Boy. Half Vampire. ALL HERO!

Bram always knew he was different, but he never imagined that he was half-vampire! Recruited into a school for kid monsters, Bram unravels his mysterious past and learns about his shocking future. He must save humanity from the terrifying return of Count Dracula!

UNLEGENDARY DRAGON Series:

A New Hero Takes Flight! Unless He Goes Down in Flames...

When Connor moves to the mystical island of Lore, he discovers his dragon-sized destiny. With the power of a magical amulet, he must shapeshift into a legendary dragon to protect the world from evil! There's just one problem—Connor has no clue how to be a dragon.

ABOUT THE AUTHOR

R.L. Ullman is the bestselling, award-winning author of books for young readers, including the EPIC ZERO® series, THE BOY WITH VIDEO GAME POWERS™ series, the UNLEGENDARY DRAGON® series, the MONSTER PROBLEMS series, and the PETUNIA THE UNICORN® series. He writes the kinds of books he loved reading as a kid, featuring fast-paced action, laugh-out-loud humor, and lots of heart. R.L. lives in Connecticut with his laptop and family. Visit rlullman.com for discounted book bundles, signed books, book merchandise, and more!

CONNECT WITH R.L.

Join R.L.'s mailing list at rlullman.com for discounts, exclusive offers, free content, and notifications about new releases! See what R.L. is working on at r.l.ullman_author on Instagram and @authorRLUllman on Facebook.

ACKNOWLEDGMENTS

Writing this book was a multiplayer effort and I couldn't have done it without my top level wife and editor, Lynn; my elite gamer son and story consultant, Matthew; and my power-boosting daughter, Olivia.

Made in the USA
Las Vegas, NV
17 December 2024

14566916R00090